'You're not **are you, N** **asked softly.**

'I'm here to work and nothing more. I can't work, though, and I can't stay if you're going to be like this all the time.'

'I'm always like this,' he assured her ironically, his eyes narrowed and watchful.

'No, you're not,' Erica muttered. 'For a minute, you looked human.'

'Trick of the light,' he said drily. 'Haven't you ever seen one of the big cats smile? It's not really smiling. It's a trick of the light.'

'I've never lived amongst wild animals,' Erica told him sharply, and Alex allowed his eyes to run over her in a way that was really alarming.

'Use your imagination,' he suggested quietly, 'and keep watching your step. I'll be here more often than not.'

Patricia Wilson was born in Yorkshire and lived there until she married and had four children. She loves travelling and has lived in Singapore, Africa and Spain. She had always wanted to be a writer but a growing family and career as a teacher left her with little time to pursue her interest. With the encouragement of her family she gave up teaching in order to concentrate on writing and her other interests of music and painting.

Recent titles by the same author:

BORROWED WIFE
AN INNOCENT CHARADE
COMING HOME

MACBRIDE'S DAUGHTER

BY
PATRICIA WILSON

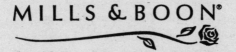

MILLS & BOON®

MILLS & BOON and MILLS & BOON with the Rose Device are registered trademarks of the publisher.

First published in Great Britain 1997
Harlequin Mills & Boon Limited,
Eton House, 18-24 Paradise Road, Richmond, Surrey TW9 1SR

© Patricia Wilson 1997

ISBN 0 263 80033 4

Set in Times Roman 10 on 12 pt.
02-9703-57150 C1

Printed and bound in Great Britain
by Mackays of Chatham PLC, Chatham

CHAPTER ONE

ERICA glanced through the windscreen and frowned at the sky. It looked heavy, full of snow, and she knew that the flurries of white that came at intervals now, blown on a rising wind, were just the advance warning of things to come. On the main roads it had not been too bad, but since she had turned onto the more narrow roads that led deeper into the cold countryside the evidence of icy conditions had become much more apparent.

Beneath the wheels of her car, the last fall of snow crunched audibly—proof that things were icing over rapidly. New snow was settling, and before too long these narrow roads would be impassable. The firm base beneath the falling snow would be ice. Driving would be dangerous.

It didn't really matter. She was almost there, and her frown deepened as she thought of the man she had been tracking down for the last few weeks. In the end, it had been surprisingly easy. After years of wondering and waiting, she would soon see him. She had taken a month's unpaid leave but it would be worth it. Before the month was out she would know what she had wanted to know for most of her life.

Not that she felt rejected and scarred by the fact that her father had left and never returned; she had not even been born then. It was impossible to feel rejected by someone who had never even seen you. All the same, he had shelved his responsibilities and now, after all the years, she knew why. He had a life that her mother had been unable to share, a life that few wives would have been willing to face, and he had kept to his own path, discarding his wife and unborn child.

It had only been in her late teens that she had begun to feel the resentment, and even now her mother did not know why the resentment was there. Erica grimaced to herself. She was twenty-four, more than able to cope with anything, but the memory of teenage suffering stayed inside—a suffering she would never have had to face if she had had her own father around.

What sort of a man would leave his child at risk? She would soon know because she had him in her sights, almost in her grasp, and he had no idea that she was closing in on him, no idea of her plans.

The country road widened and she gave a sigh of relief, allowing a little more speed. She had to be there before nightfall because after that the place would be difficult to find. She had the village and the name of the house but she had never been so far north before and after a life spent in the city the darkening countryside looked bleak and just a little menacing. It would have been best to stop and spend the night in some hotel but Erica had been too eager to arrive, too eager to put her plan into action.

Without warning there were roadworks, cones, flashing amber lights and the road was suddenly down to the width of one car. A glance at the side of the road showed her that a long trench was being dug and even the surface of the part of the road left open was rutted and uneven.

Erica's lips tightened in annoyance. Typical! Not one warning sign, not one indication that a road was to become a feeble, bumpy track. The snow was sticking to the windscreen, trying to defeat the efforts of the wipers, and on the headlights it was succeeding very well. They seemed dim and inadequate, more snow coating them before the heat of the lights could melt off the last attack of white.

Suddenly, there was a jolting thump as one wheel hit a deep hole. The car went on but it slewed to the side and Erica had to fight the wheel to keep straight. She didn't need to stop and get out to know what had happened. Some great hole had been left for the unwary and she had hit it. Her tyre would be flat; her whole wheel might even be damaged. All the same, she couldn't stop here.

The end of the cones appeared in her headlights and she kept on, creeping forward, ignoring the damage she was compounding. Stopping in the narrowed lane would have been dangerous both for herself and any other driver coming later. She pulled into the side of the road as soon as it widened and she was too angry even to consider her predicament.

She was stuck here at the back of beyond but her annoyance overshadowed every other thought. Roadworks, cones, damned great holes! She lived with them daily, and even here in this place at the end of the world men were digging like so many demented rodents and then going off happily, leaving sufficient problems to puzzle the driver of a tank!

Erica climbed out, pulling the collar of her jacket closely around her. It seemed natural to get out and look, though what she would do after that was anybody's guess. Sure enough, the front nearside tyre was as flat as the proverbial pancake and the irritated kick that she aimed at it with one slim, booted foot did nothing to correct the situation.

She looked around in the gathering dusk. As far as the eye could see there was nothing. There were trees, already coated with white, hedges and fields that were rapidly losing their sharp contours and it was getting dark. This was Northumberland, reputed for its beauty and magnificent seascapes, but right at this moment she would have given anything for the sight of a dirty street with one telephone kiosk.

She hugged her jacket close, already feeling the warmth fading. Before long she would be shivering with cold and she had no idea how far she was from her destination. The chance of rescue here was small and she was not too happy about the prospect of a walk through dark, narrow lanes with a snowstorm gathering strength by the minute. She gazed at the wheel in frustration and then lifted startled, thankful eyes to the approaching lights of another car.

Don't let him hit that hole, she prayed fervently. Just let at least one of us have transport out of here.

It was only as the car passed, slowing all the time, that any thought of danger entered her mind. The car reversed towards her, and when the engine died and silence drifted back across the landscape Erica realised once again how far from civilisation she was.

Her own headlights were still on and they caught the other car in their beam. It was a bigger car, a silver Mercedes as far as she could tell, but that didn't preclude the driver from being a raving lunatic who had spotted her as a victim. Her relief became tinged with caution and Erica watched carefully as the driver got out and closed his door. It was too dark and there was too much snow for her to see him clearly, however much she tried.

It was then that her eyes wavered and fastened on the object she could see against his back window. Tossed there carelessly, it was now well illuminated by her headlights, a Day-Glo jacket that seemed to be looking at her smugly. The very sight of it said 'Roadworks' in her mind and all her fury returned.

And he was not just some man who dug mindless holes and waved 'stop' signs at hurrying travellers. Oh, no! She had never seen one of them climb into a Mercedes to eat his sandwiches. This one was worse. This was one of the men who gave the orders. This one would have drawn a cross on the map of a perfectly respectable road and said, 'Dig here.'

What was he doing now? Had he come to see who was caught in the trap? Erica saw red. All anxiety left her and she glared at him as he approached. She still couldn't see him properly but she didn't much care if he was eight feet tall.

'What do you intend to do about this?' she blazed, pointing at her sad-looking tyre.

He stopped, narrowing his eyes against the glare of her headlights and the driving snow, trying to see her, and he had the cheek to look mystified—she could make that out now.

'Surely you're not surprised?' she raged. 'I can hardly be the first victim and most certainly I won't be the last, especially on a night like this. How dare you allow these holes to be left unguarded? This may be a small road but it is a road all the same. Drivers have rights too. The roads don't belong entirely to people who have control of diggers and bulldozers.'

It was quite a speech and as she stopped for breath he stood and regarded her silently. His face looked as cold as the weather and she could see that he was dark-

haired. Snow was settling on his hair but he had ignored
it so far. He was wearing dark trousers and a thick,
warm-looking high-necked sweater, and although he had
not bothered with a coat he looked a good deal warmer
than Erica now felt.

'What makes you imagine I have any authority over
roadworks?' he asked icily.

'Who else would have authority?' she snapped, irritated further by his acidly superior tone. 'It's typical that
once permission is given for a few men to dig a lot of
holes all responsibility is cast aside. You drive about
looking important, boldly entering roads with no access
for ordinary people. You put down millions of hideous
cones that restrict everyone else and after that you do
nothing at all!' Erica had come forward angrily to deliver this lecture and now she pointed at the jacket visible
against his back window. 'Roadworks engineers are in
a category of their own!'

She glared up at him and waited for his excuses but
his next action alarmed her considerably. He stepped
forward and took her arm in a very punishing grip as
he marched her to the front of his car. Except for the
one sentence he had not said a word and he said nothing
now. He simply pointed at the windscreen of the
Mercedes, and in the gathering darkness Erica saw a
sticker. 'Doctor—Accident Emergency Unit.'

She was horrified. Waves of dreadful embarrassment
began to wash over her and his grip on her arm tightened as he marched her back to the rear door of his car
and opened it. If he had been about to push her inside
and kidnap her she would have been too filled with shame
to resist but he reached in and pulled out the jacket that
had so enraged her. As before he said nothing at all. He
simply jerked it out and shook it open, releasing her arm

to tap at the word on the back of the jacket with one irritated finger. It said 'DOCTOR.'

For a second she was stunned by her own foolish assumptions and outrageous behaviour and he stared at her unwaveringly, dark-eyed and extremely irritated.

'I'm sorry,' she gulped. 'I really had no right to—to go on at you like that, even if you had been a roadworks engineer. I suppose it was because I was scared, being stranded out here.'

'You were not stranded from the moment I arrived,' he pointed out coldly. 'As to being scared, I find that impossible to envisage. It's probably just as well that I have nothing to do with repairing roads. Otherwise we might have been here all night while I explained my inexcusable conduct.'

Erica was well aware of her own inexcusable conduct but she didn't get the chance to apologise further. He had not been impressed by her first attempt and she had the feeling that any further offers of abject misery about her behaviour would merely annoy him more. He walked off to her car and left her standing there.

When she caught up with him he was crouching down to look at her flat tyre, and that made her feel worse than ever.

'It's quite all right,' she muttered feebly. 'I can manage. I—I hadn't even stopped to ask for help when I thought you were a roadworks engineer.'

'I'm well aware of that,' he grunted irascibly. 'You were waiting here to rage at any man unfortunate enough to possess a Day-Glo jacket.' He stood up, towering over her, glancing at the sky with the same irritation that he was showing her. 'This snow is about to get much worse. If you would be so kind as to open the boot, I'll get your spare wheel and change it for you. You can then be on your way while it's still possible to drive.'

Erica looked at him a little warily and he stared back, one dark brow raised in question when she didn't immediately obey his orders.

'The spare wheel,' he repeated, as if she might just be slightly stupid and unable to comprehend English at that level.

'I haven't really got one,' Erica confessed in a shamefaced manner. 'The tyre wanted changing on the spare wheel and I—well, I . . .'

'The last time I heard,' he rasped, 'it was against the law to travel without a suitable spare wheel.'

'I meant to get it fixed,' Erica pleaded uncomfortably, 'but I was in too much of a hurry and—'

'Which seems to bring us to the fact that I'm stuck with you.'

He stared at her angrily, his dark eyes running over her with very obvious exasperation. She was huddled in a fashionable jacket with a fake-fur-trimmed collar, and although her legs were enclosed in trousers and high boots it was easy to see that they were aimed at fashion only, with no consideration given to warmth and severe weather.

The snow was settling on her dark hair and she couldn't quite manage to suppress the shiver that the cold forced on her. He muttered to himself in great irritation and before she had quite recovered from her shivering attack she was being marched back to the Mercedes.

He opened the door, indicating that she should get inside, but Erica was too embarrassed to obey.

'There really is no need...' she began, but he glared at her furiously, his black brows drawn into a quite alarming frown.

'I've had enough emergencies for one night,' he snapped. 'I have no intention of being called out again when you are found huddled in your car with hypothermia.'

He almost thrust her inside the warmth of his car, strode back to wrench her suitcases out of her own vehicle and slammed them onto his back seat. Before she could gather her wits they were moving. Her car had been locked, the lights had been put out, her keys tossed onto her lap, and it was now abandoned to the snow and the night. She hardly dared settle into the welcome warmth because she could feel annoyance simmering in the man beside her and she felt about one inch tall, greatly subdued.

The wind had risen even more and they were driving through swirling snow that would quite obviously get much worse before very long, and Erica knew that without his aid she would have been in a very sorry state.

'Where are you going?'

He suddenly shot the question at her and Erica glanced across at him a little anxiously. He would be even more annoyed when he realised she was going to make him go a long way from his own destination.

'East Winton. It's a little village not too far away but I think it's not easy to reach.'

He just grunted and she knew she had antagonised him to the limit of his endurance. She was quite capable of antagonising people at the best of times and this was not the best of times at all.

'If it's out of your way...' she ventured in a subdued voice.

'Not really. I live there.'

'Oh, do you? That's good,' Erica said cheerfully with some attempt to lighten the atmosphere and possibly placate him. 'You'll probably know Keresford House, then? That's where I'm going.'

'Why?'

The abrupt question stopped Erica's attempts at conciliation. Obviously it would not be possible to negotiate a truce with this man. She gave some slight consideration to telling him that it was her business and none of his but he had rescued her after being soundly berated for nothing. In the second place, now that she was sitting beside him and not blinded by snow, she could see that he was not in any way a weakling. He might decide to forsake his medical oath and push her out of the car into the cold darkness.

'I'm going to act as a secretary to Mr Macbride. He's writing his memoirs and I'm going to help him. I'm expecting to be there for about a month, depending on how it goes, of course. Apparently he's already made copious notes and worked everything out so it should be pretty straightforward.'

He shot her a disbelieving look and she couldn't tell whether she was talking too much or whether he thought she was utterly incapable of having the brains and the drive necessary to work at all.

He made no comment whatever and Erica decided that it was best to be silent too. There was a very bad atmosphere in the car. If he had been the sort of man she liked he would have been laughing at her attack, very amused now that it was over. He wasn't even vaguely amused and it seemed that everything she said made him worse. In the circumstances, therefore, silence appeared to be a good idea.

She peered through the windscreen, watching the heavy, swirling snow. There was nothing to see really and she wondered if he was finding his way by some instinct. If he lived and worked here, though, he probably knew every tree and rock. There hadn't seemed to be much more than that in the landscape when she had been able to see and her mind went longingly back to heat and warmth, the sun and sea.

She would have been there by now, in Singapore, if she hadn't been on this particular voyage of discovery. Erica wondered if the irritated man beside her had picked up her vibes when she had told him such a hearty lie. She was not a secretary at all. She could type very well and she was methodical so, as far as anyone knew, she could easily be a secretary, but it was not how she lived.

Erica was an airline stewardess and her flight would just about be landing in Singapore now. Not only was this a month of unpaid leave, it would probably be the most traumatic month of her life. She frowned and shut down the particular chain of thought. Nothing could have been more traumatic than her teenage years.

This was where she paid back. This was where she demanded explanations. Everything seemed to have played into her hands: the advertisement she had seen at just the right time, the ease with which she had been accepted, even the fact that this disgruntled male had rescued her when she was so close to her goal. It all seemed to be an omen. It must be, and after this she would get on with her life and forget the whole thing.

They came to lights, not many of them but enough for Erica to see that they had reached a village. In the shelter of the houses and the tall trees that grew around a village square the snow was not as bad. The place was pretty, beautiful even, and as Erica glanced around her she saw the sign on the little post office at the side of the road. 'East Winton'. The few lights lit up the sign. She had arrived.

Suddenly, the enormity of her undertaking hit her and she wondered how she had ever contemplated this move. She was going to see her father and, according to her mother, he didn't even know that she existed. He was fifty years old now, again according to her mother. For all that time he had not known about her. He might have a family of his own—sons, daughters—people who would not be too pleased at her intrusion.

Erica pulled herself together. She was not going to march in and demand explanations at once. She had covered her tracks well and she didn't intend to say one word until she had discovered exactly what sort of man her father was. Nobody would even suspect that she was anything other than a secretary who had answered his advertisement and if she simply hated it at the house she would leave and forget the whole thing at once with no waiting at all.

They were driving from the village now, and once again Erica had a slight attack of nerves. The address had said 'Keresford House, East Winton' and yet they were leaving East Winton behind.

'Er—that was the village, East Winton,' she pointed out a trifle anxiously.

'So it was,' her dark rescuer drawled ironically. 'I thought it looked familiar.'

'But you live there!' Erica reminded him, her eyes noting again that he was a tall, muscular-looking man who had come as a stranger into her life. She had taken everything he said on trust and, looking back, she realised he had not given her much alternative.

'Not exactly,' he corrected her. 'I live outside the village, not in it.' He shot her a very sardonic look. 'Surely you're not beginning to fear for your life? Your tongue is a very lethal weapon and, used with your skill, it would probably stop a whole company of villains.'

'I was merely confused,' Erica told him huffily, assuring herself that if he had wanted to attack her he had already had ample opportunity. Anyway, he was a doctor. That made him respectable.

She had the nasty feeling that he was enjoying her apprehension. He had certainly heard the disquiet in her voice. It didn't say a lot for his bedside manner. Who on earth would want a sarcastic doctor who was amused by his patients' fear? Not that he looked amused. She could only see his profile but it looked like well-carved rock.

The car turned off the road and her nerves came rushing back to the surface at the sight of tall trees and fences topped with an inch or more of snow. Where was he taking her? She looked at him with open anxiety and he glanced at her as he felt her eyes on him.

'This is the drive of Keresford House,' he assured her quietly. 'In a minute, you'll see the lights.'

'Thank you,' Erica said shakily. 'I—I wondered where we were.'

'Quite within screaming distance if the car should break down,' he muttered irritably, and she knew for sure that he had picked up her agitation. Not that she would have had much chance to scream if he had turned out to be a villain after all. She could still feel the grip he had used on her arm when he had marched her to his car. He would make a good doctor for a wrestler. He would probably break a person's bones as he examined them.

The house came into sight at that moment and Erica bit down hard on her lip, all her misgivings returning with a rush. It looked very beautiful, a picture, the lights gleaming from the windows showing the fallen snow that already carpeted the wide lawns. The house was much, much bigger than she had visualised and the tall chimneys were just discernible against the dark, snowy sky.

'Keresford House,' her dark companion said quietly, and Erica was extremely glad to hear his voice. She had been sinking into a state of panic at her own temerity.

'It's beautiful,' she ventured softly, and he gave a sort of grunt of agreement.

'Quite beautiful in daylight. It's Victorian. There are fourteen acres of grounds. If you have time off from your secretarial duties you'll be able to look around, providing that you actually intend to stay here.'

'That was the agreement,' Erica said quickly. 'Mr Macbride wants a secretary to live in until he's finished his book.'

'He mentioned it to me. Somehow, though, I don't think he's quite expecting a secretary like you.'

'There's nothing wrong with me!' Erica snapped, feeling a little more secure now that the car had stopped in front of the house.

'Of course not,' he drawled in his infuriating manner. 'I'll warn Philip to hide any Day-Glo jacket he has and everything will be fine.'

'I've apologised for my mistake,' Erica reminded him sharply, and he just shot her a look that would have turned a weak person to stone. He was back to saying nothing, however, and as he got out of the car Erica followed suit, glad that she would soon be in the warm house, whatever its dangers.

He collected her luggage and walked to the steps and Erica rushed forward, intent on stopping him right then and breaking off any further contact.

'I can see to the cases myself,' she managed a trifle breathlessly. 'Thank you for helping me, but there's no reason why you shouldn't leave me here now and—and get—'

'And get about my business?' he interrupted sardonically. He looked down at her in the lights from the entrance porch and she was startled to see how tall he really was, how dark his hair and how dark his eyes. He was extremely handsome too but he was as hard as nails. If she had been able to see him more clearly when she had set about him on the lonely road she would have behaved a little more cautiously.

'I didn't say that,' she reminded him quietly. 'I just don't want to put you to any more trouble.'

'No trouble.' He just walked forward with her cases, ignoring her obvious desire to see the last of him. 'I'm going here anyway.'

'Oh,' Erica said with audible disappointment. 'You're visiting.'

'In a manner of speaking,' he assured her, not even bothering to turn round. 'I'm expecting to be fed too. I live here. In fact, this is my house.'

'Mr Macbride said... In his letter he said... This is the address!' Erica panicked and he turned then and looked down at her with decidedly malicious amusement.

'This is indeed the address,' he assured her. 'Philip Macbride is my stepfather.' He gave her a very tight-lipped smile. 'He married my mother all of twenty years ago. When she died, he came back home and moved in with me.'

'So—so you always live here?' Erica muttered miserably, almost abandoning her plan right then.

'Naturally. It's my house. Shall we go inside now? I wouldn't want to see you shivering again.'

It was too late. She was shivering now and it wasn't just the cold. She *loathed* this man. He was so arrogant and so bad-tempered. She wouldn't last here a day.

'I—I'm Erica Linton,' she ventured anxiously, and he just nodded and turned to the door, carrying her heavy cases with no effort at all.

'I know,' he said quietly. 'I read your letter of application and all those wonderful qualifications.'

All those wonderful lies. He didn't say it but it was there in his voice. Even the back of his dark head looked disbelieving and disapproving. She was going to have to try very hard to get along with him if she was staying in the same house. *His* house.

'I don't even know your name,' she began uneasily, and he opened the door, putting her cases down and standing aside for her to enter.

'Thorne,' he said coolly. 'Alex Thorne.'

Erica nodded, biting at her lip and looking away hastily. His introducing himself didn't make things any better. She would probably have fled there and then if she had not been stranded. It was going to be tricky enough pretending to be a secretary and summing up her father, without having this tall, powerful man watching her every move with suspicion.

She almost gasped as another unwelcome thought hit her. If Philip Macbride was her father and this was his stepson, then—then ... She stared up at him in horror and found his dark eyes inspecting her closely, from her dark red hair and deep blue eyes to her slender figure.

'Oh!' she muttered, unable to stop the sound of dread that entered her voice.

'You're probably right,' he agreed sardonically. 'Come into the drawing room. I'll get Philip to come and cope with you.'

His tone said clearly that he had coped with her for quite long enough and she was very glad that his sarcastic comment about her shocked muttering had been made simply out of lingering annoyance. He certainly didn't know what she knew. Alex Thorne—Dr Thorne—was her stepbrother, and Erica thought with terrible longing of her little car and its fate.

She had already had dreadful thoughts about her father's having a family of his own but she had never imagined that she would be stuck here trying to play her unusual role with the dark, cold eyes of a stepbrother on her. She had the feeling that he was fond of her father. If she made one wrong move she could expect no mercy at all, medical oath or not.

Alex Thorne was a ready-made enemy, and she had the feeling that even if she had not antagonised him right from the first she was just the sort of person he would dislike on sight. She had not missed the way he had been inspecting her. There had been contempt in his eyes as he had summed up her appearance and her clothes. He thought she was some idiotic social butterfly. He probably thought she was doing this job for a lark.

Whatever he thought, she would have to stick it out, and Erica's lips set stubbornly as she followed him across a wide, carpeted hall to the tall doors of the drawing room. She was not about to let one unpleasant male put her off. She had finished with unpleasant males and the fact that she had been forced to put up with any unpleasant male at all was entirely her father's fault. She

had come here to get him, finally to confront him with
his sins, and that was exactly what she would do. Dr
Thorne could stare at her coldly for the whole month.
It didn't make one bit of difference.

CHAPTER TWO

THE drawing room was huge, with a bright, cheerful fire burning in the grate of a lovely old fireplace. It was a very comfortable, welcoming room and Erica felt a wave of something quite akin to dismay. There had been nothing welcoming about her own home. Modern, functional and very suburban, it had occupied her mother's life to the exclusion of most other things. This room, whilst being on the verge of luxurious, was still a room that was very much lived in.

Two great settees flanked the fireplace and various easy chairs were scattered around the room. There were several pieces in beautiful dark wood which looked like antiques—tables, bookcases, a writing bureau and, in the corner, a baby grand piano that gleamed in the light from the fire and the lamps.

A big, very lazy-looking black Labrador got slowly to its feet as they entered the room but didn't seem to want to actually leave the soft rug by the fire.

'Come on, boy. What about a greeting?' Alex Thorne said with more warmth than Erica had so far heard, and the dog began to wag its tail as it finally decided to come forward.

'This is Charlie.' The dark eyes flashed briefly to Erica's face as she stood there uncertainly. 'Say hello to Miss Linton, Charlie. She's staying here so it's no use pretending you don't see her.'

It was a nasty little dig and quite indicative of the state of his mind but Erica studiously disregarded him. The dog came up to her enquiringly and she held out her hand to it.

'You can call me Erica,' she assured it haughtily. 'I don't always allow such intimacy but I'll make an exception with you.'

To her surprise, Alex Thorne's lips twitched in amusement, and she quickly ignored him as she bent to pat the dog on the head. The arrogant doctor was not going to get away with this kind of irritating and belittling behaviour. He must have approved of his stepfather's decision to have a secretary living in the house and if he didn't like the one he was stuck with then it was his bad luck.

'Come up to the fire.' Erica looked up and found that once again the dark eyes were summing her up. 'You look cold. I'll get Philip and then he can tell you your duties and make arrangements for your stay here.'

'I thought he might not be in,' Erica murmured as she slipped back from defiance to anxiety at the thought of meeting the man who had left so long ago.

'He's lived in Africa for most of his life,' Alex Thorne told her, his eyes still assessing her appearance. 'I would put the chance of Philip being out on a night like this at zero.'

At the mention of Africa, Erica showed no surprise; in fact she nodded in understanding, and at once the dark eyes narrowed and became more intent.

'You don't seem to be startled at the thought of my stepfather's unusual past, Miss Linton,' he said coolly. 'I assume you know the sort of book he's writing?'

'His memoirs. That's what he said in his letter. I imagine it's going to be exciting, about his life on a game reserve.'

'Do you?' Alex Thorne asked icily. 'How astute of you. I don't recall that he mentioned his past at all in his letter to you.'

'Well, he must have done or I wouldn't know,' Erica said quickly, frantically trying to remember whether her father had said anything about his past or if she had spoken from the knowledge that her talks with her mother had given her.

'You're here because he can't type at all,' Alex Thorne reminded her. 'As his handwriting is diabolical and utterly illegible to the uninitiated, I typed out his letter to you. I remember it quite clearly. There was no mention of his past at all.'

'I read it in the paper. I'd forgotten. It was some time ago.' Erica corrected herself in a rush, horrified to find that her cheeks were beginning to flush guiltily.

'But it all came back to you when you read his advertisement?' Alex Thorne queried coldly. 'You were taking a chance, Miss Linton, coming to an isolated house to work for a man you didn't know. Was it the lure of Africa?'

Erica had run out of excuses and he stared at her unwaveringly, reminding her of a rather dangerous animal waiting to attack. She almost cried out with relief when another person entered the room and the suspicious stare was replaced by a smile as Alex looked up to greet the newcomer.

'I've brought your secretary, Philip,' he said wryly. 'I found her stranded and shivering in the snow. We introduced ourselves at once and it became apparent that she was coming here.'

Sarcasm was heavy in his voice and Erica disliked him more with each passing second. He was not about to give a blow-by-blow account of her attack on him but he was going to remind her of it constantly.

'Miss Linton! I'm so glad you managed to get here. You couldn't have chosen a worse night to arrive. It's lucky that Alex was able to rescue you. It can be quite dangerous up here when the snow comes.'

Erica turned round slowly, fighting to control her expression. After all these years she was going to see her father and the bitterness rushed back with a speed that astounded her. Here, in this comfortable room, in this lovely house with every sign of wealth and ease, it didn't seem fair that he should have left her to the mercy of the man who had married her mother.

She knew all about stepfathers, but she had not been a tall, powerful man like Alex Thorne. She had been a tiny little girl and then a slender, helpless teenager. Her blue eyes were cold as she turned to look at the man who had abandoned her to that.

His appearance shocked her out of her bitterness and she had to remind herself hastily that he was only fifty years old. He looked much older and he looked ill. His skin had been darkened by years in the sun but the tan he must have had for most of his life had faded into a sort of buff colour as if there was no health behind the skin. He was tall—not as tall as Alex Thorne—but he was painfully thin, and though the eyes that looked at her were as deeply blue as her own they were dark-rimmed and faded with some sort of suffering.

Her stepfather was fifty also but Jack Linton's physique was tough, powerful, with the force and energy of the bully behind his every action. Philip Macbride looked as if a trip up the stairs that she had seen as she'd come through the hall would just about finish him off.

It was impossible to imagine him on some game reserve, working in the sun, bronzed and fit.

'I—I'm very glad to have arrived safely,' she managed to say, trying very hard not to stare too pointedly. 'I don't know what I would have done if Dr Thorne hadn't come along at the right time—'

'You would have stopped the next motorist,' Alex Thorne cut in smoothly. 'That particular road is well used; it leads directly from the road that runs off the motorway. Of course, it looked like a rough track, but I can assure you that they'll get it finished—and move on to another place.'

Erica flashed him a furious glance and he looked back at her blandly. Was he never going to stop with this irritating innuendo? The sooner she was out of his sight the better. The dog decided to lick her hand and she glanced down gratefully. She had almost reached the stage where she dared not say anything at all.

'I'll get Mrs Roberts to take you to your room,' Philip Macbride said. 'We can talk at dinner and tomorrow I'll show you my little study. It's cosy. I'm sure we'll be able to get along speedily with the manuscript. I feel quite excited about it.'

'Don't overdo it, Philip,' Alex Thorne said suddenly, and Erica saw his dark glance move to her father as he gave him a careful inspection. For the first time, he looked like a doctor and with that came a feeling that was almost hysterical relief. She didn't know why it should be so but for that moment he didn't look either threatening or cruel. He just looked caring, and the change was astonishing. He looked the sort of man you could take your problems to.

'Can't overdo it sitting down and talking,' Philip Macbride pointed out cheerfully, and Alex Thorne nodded although he still looked doubtful.

'I'll be watching you,' he warned. Her father led her to the door and Alex added, 'I'll bring your cases up, Miss Linton. Just leave them there in the hall.'

He sounded tired, and at the sound of his voice Philip Macbride turned and looked at him closely.

'Was it bad?' he asked quietly.

'No more than usual. Two in hospital, one dead.'

And Erica suddenly knew where he had been coming from when she had encountered him and set upon him. The motorway was not more than two miles from where she had been stranded. He had gone out to answer an emergency call and come back to be waylaid and attacked by a madwoman. She was so sorry, so ashamed that she just stood there and looked at him woefully.

He looked up and noticed her expression, his brows raised questioningly.

'I—I didn't know,' she said regretfully. 'I didn't know you'd been . . .'

'I don't normally wave a banner,' he assured her drily. His lips tilted in a quizzical half-smile. 'Meeting you served to clear my mind, however, so don't be too dismayed. Think of it as your little bit of public service.'

He turned away, dismissing her, and Erica followed her father from the room. She felt totally inadequate and very lost. What was she doing here? She didn't belong here. This man who walked in front of her to the hall had not even known of her existence and she should leave at once and forget this whole mad plan. If her car had been parked outside she would have left immediately and let them think just whatever they wanted but she was stuck here, at least for the night.

The huge, quiet, warm house was outside her experience. Her father was a stranger—a sick stranger. She didn't need to be a doctor to know that. As for the doctor in question, he was the sort of man she had never come into contact with before, not even on her many flights to exotic places.

Of course, being a doctor, he worked, and probably worked very hard, but at the moment Erica felt very much the ordinary working girl. He seemed to be some towering being who stared down at her and thought of her with a certain amount of suspicion and a good deal of contempt.

Her father stopped as a woman came into the hall from one of the other rooms. She was middle-aged and to Erica's relief she looked kindly and motherly.

'Ah! Mrs Roberts. This is my new secretary,' her father said proudly, as if he had suddenly become extremely important. He was almost boyish, and in spite of her grim thoughts Erica felt a smile begin to edge her lips.

'You must be Miss Linton,' the housekeeper said, beaming at her. 'We've been expecting you. Your room's all ready. I'll take you up. What a night to arrive. We might just be snowed in by morning.'

Erica hoped not. By morning she might need to escape, and she thought anxiously about her car. When she came back down she would have to mention it. She would ask where the nearest garage was and maybe get them to collect it, repair the wheel and then deliver it here. If she could manage that she would not be at the mercy of anyone at all.

'Leave the cases, Mrs Roberts. I'll bring them up,' the familiar dark voice said from the doorway of the drawing room, and Mrs Roberts nodded her approval as she led Erica up the wide, open staircase.

'You'll find that Dr Thorne is a very kind man,' she confided quietly to Erica. 'There's no need at all for him to do what he's been doing tonight. He volunteered to be on call for accidents and I wouldn't like to think how many lives that saves, with people driving like madmen even on nights like this. I suppose he's used to it in some ways but now and again he looks completely shattered when he gets back, especially when there's been somebody he couldn't save. He looks tired tonight.'

It drove the arrow of guilt even further into Erica and she was glad when the housekeeper stopped at a door on the passage upstairs and opened it with a smile, gesturing for Erica to step inside.

'This is a lovely room. I think it's just about my favourite. When Miss Fiona comes—that's Dr Thorne's cousin—she's always trying to wheedle her way to having this room but it's not really for an overnight guest and she never stays for long. We thought it might be just right for you because you'll be here for a while and this room is big enough to give you some privacy.'

It was certainly big and Erica was quite taken aback. Of course, this room had been picked out for her father's secretary long before Alex Thorne had known she was a bad-tempered maniac. If he had been aware of her tendencies he would have put a tent up for her on the lawn, or even in the vegetable garden.

'It's beautiful,' she said, and Mrs Roberts gave her another beam of approval.

'Well, you've got your own bathroom and there's this bit here by the window with its own settee and chair like a little sitting room. Dr Thorne brought this small desk up for you and put it right by the window in the light. He wanted you to feel at home because it's very important for Mr Macbride to get on with his book. He's a sick man and this has cheered him up no end. We wouldn't want you to feel uncomfortable and decide to leave. Mr Macbride has been all on edge waiting for you to come.'

She looked at Erica closely and then smiled and nodded. 'You look nice and kind, quiet—just what Mr Macbride needs. He hasn't to be upset in any way at all but I can see that you're perfect for his secretary. He'll get on with you a treat.'

She bustled out and Erica sat on the end of the bed and gave a big sigh. What had she walked into? She had come here like an avenger with a drawn sword and instead of finding a hard, callous man she had found an invalid. He had no family of his own apparently, but that didn't mean he was unprotected. From Alex Thorne's attitude and the attitude of Mrs Roberts it was clear that if she put one foot out of line she would be savaged.

It had all been a very bad mistake, one she regretted. It wasn't possible to look at her father and feel any anger. He was too ill for that. She had no idea what was wrong with him but it must be something bad. She had imagined him all wrongly, her idea of a man of his age very much coloured by her memories of Jack Linton. There was not even the slightest comparison and now she felt incredibly out of place here and she would never confront her father with any crime at all.

There was a knock on the door and she turned her head as Alex Thorne came in with her cases. She had felt too dejected to get up but now she sprang to her feet and looked at him warily. Would he start again, questioning her about her uncanny knowledge of her father's past?

'I'll put them here,' he said, setting her cases at the end of the bed as Erica jumped back speedily. 'If there's anything you want, just let Mrs Roberts know.'

'Does she live in too?' Erica asked, breaking into speech rather than allowing him to start questioning her again.

'Cottage in the grounds,' he murmured, lifting her last case to the bed. 'It dates from the days when this was a rather grand house and boasted a gamekeeper.'

'It's a rather grand house now,' she pointed out, and he looked at her quizzically.

'I'm glad you approve. At one point downstairs I gained the distinct impression that you were about to race off into the snowy night and disappear from sight.'

'I felt embarrassed,' Erica confessed quietly. 'I raged at you for nothing and quite obviously you could have done without that after—after...'

'Unfortunate,' he muttered, turning away, and she could see that he had not wanted to be reminded about his rescue attempts. 'In any case,' he added, just as she was beginning to relax, 'quite clearly your clairvoyant abilities don't cover everything. You did remarkably well with Philip's past even though you had never seen him. I should think that being an oracle once a day is enough to wear you out.'

Erica just looked at him. There wasn't really anything she could say, and he stared back at her inflexibly.

'You're not quite what you seem, are you, Miss Linton?' he asked softly. 'But that's all right. Just remember, though, that I'll be watching you as much as I'll be watching my stepfather. He's a sick man and he's by no means on the road to recovery yet. Nothing must upset that recovery. He came home to get better and that's just what he'll do. Of course, you probably saw all that in your vision so there's no real need for me to tell you, is there?'

'I'll do nothing to upset him,' she said in a tight voice. 'I'm here to work and nothing more. I can't work, though, and I can't stay if you're going to be like this all the time.'

'I'm always like this,' he assured her ironically, his eyes narrowed and watchful.

'No you're not,' Erica muttered. 'For a minute down there, you looked human.'

'Trick of the light,' he said drily. 'Haven't you ever seen one of the big cats smile? It's not really smiling. It's a trick of the light.'

'I've never lived amongst wild animals,' Erica told him sharply, and Erica allowed his eyes to run over her in a way that was really alarming.

'Use your imagination,' he suggested quietly, 'and keep watching your step. I'll be here more often than not.'

Before she could think of a suitable retort he had walked out, closing the door behind him in an unnaturally quiet manner, and Erica sat back down with a thump. She had the awful feeling that he knew all about her but, of course, he didn't. How could he? Even her mother hadn't known her plans. She had told no one at all. The only person who knew she was coming here was Jeremy and she hadn't even told him why.

She made a frantic note in her mind to phone him tomorrow and tell him not to get in touch with her. From now on, she would be cautious all the time. Her days of attacking first and thinking later were very much numbered. Alex Thorne would retaliate and she had the uneasy feeling that any retaliation would be ferocious.

What to wear for dinner was a problem. Were they so comfortable that they didn't bother to change for the evening meal or were they so wealthy that it was normal to appear at dinner formally? There was not much chance of finding out and Erica decided to go about halfway.

She was very reluctant to unpack. Her plans now seemed to have been abandoned. All the same, she was stuck here for a while because even if her car was to be rescued tomorrow there would probably be some delay in delivering it to her because of the snow.

She peered out of the window. The lights from the house still spread across the lawn to trees at what looked like the beginning of a small stretch of parkland. It was like a Christmas card. The snow was falling heavily, being caught by the wind to swirl around the lights in clouds of feathery white. If it continued until morning there would be no way out of here until the roads and the drive were cleared.

Alex Thorne was a doctor. He would always have to be able to get out. The thought cheered her up. If he could drive out of here she could follow in his tracks—not quite like the page with Good King Wenceslas but with some measure of stealth, long after he had left. The thought of sneaking off annoyed her. His attitude was backing her into a corner and he really had nothing at all to do with her mission here. It was just unfortunate that she found herself in his house.

Erica decided to leave most of the unpacking until she had more chance to review the situation. She sorted out her clothes for dinner and then went for a nice hot shower. It was almost seven. The darkness had come early on this cold, November evening and it must have been a long time since she was saved from her icy fate by the arrival of Alex Thorne.

She felt as if she needed some safe barrier against him, and although armour would have been preferable Erica had only her clothes, her make-up and a certain amount of defiance. Even that last was dwindling rapidly and when she finally came back into the bedroom and sat down to make her face up she realised that her stay here, however short, would be quite distressing if her host was about to keep up his attacks.

The desire to linger in her room was very strong but when she was ready Erica made her way slowly down the stairs, hoping she had not chosen an inappropriate state of dress. If Alex Thorne was still wearing his thick high-necked sweater and cords she would feel rather foolish. She caught sight of herself in a long mirror in the hall and felt a little more assured.

Her long pleated skirt was bronze, matching her dainty flat shoes. She was wearing a black fine wool sweater, a gleaming bronze belt combining the two garments and showing her very slender figure. The skirt swirled silkily around her ankles as she walked and at any other time she would have been pleased with her appearance but right now she was so unsure of herself that if they all stared at her and laughed she would not have been at all surprised.

As she came to the door of the drawing room she hesitated, very grateful when Philip Macbride chose that time to appear himself.

'Go right in, Miss Linton,' he invited cheerfully. 'Alex and I usually wait in here until Mrs Roberts tells us dinner is ready. It shouldn't be long. You're probably hungry after your long journey.'

'I am,' Erica confessed, turning to smile at him. 'I was in too much of a rush to stop for any lunch. I was rather late in leaving London and it wasn't long before I began to suspect that this snow would come. I didn't

know what the weather would be like up here so I just
kept going.'

'Missing a meal can bring one quite a few unpleasant
side effects,' Alex Thorne commented. 'Low blood sugar
can cause fainting spells; at the very least, it can bring
on an unusual attack of bad temper.'

Erica lips tightened in annoyance at this instant return
to battle. He was standing by the fireplace, a drink in
his hand, and once again he was inspecting her closely.
The light caught the shine of her long dark red hair. She
had had it fastened back earlier but now it was loose
around her shoulders, slightly waving and emphasising
the deep blue of her eyes.

Alex Thorne had changed too, the thick sweater and
cords discarded for fawn trousers and a fine woollen
sweater to match. His dark hair now seemed to be darker
still and those watchful eyes seemed almost black.

'Come in,' he continued as she just stood there uneasily. 'What would you like to drink, Miss Linton?'

'Sherry, please.' She turned to her father, who was
viewing the whole proceedings with a pleased smile. It
was quite obvious that he had not even begun to suspect
that there was a good deal of animosity between his
stepson and his new secretary. 'If you would like to call
me Erica...' she began quietly, and Philip Macbride
beamed his approval at her instantly.

'Very good,' he pronounced happily. 'I can see that
we're going to get on very well indeed.'

'Here's your drink—Erica,' Alex Thorne murmured,
bringing a glass of sherry across to her. 'I hope this intimacy of using your first name extends to me? Of
course, if it's just for Philip and the dog you can tell me
right away. I'm rarely offended.'

'Let the poor girl get to the fire,' her father laughed when Erica was too angry to reply. 'You never know when to stop, Alex. It must have been a very unusual meeting when you rescued Erica. You normally let people get settled before you tear them apart.'

To Erica's surprise, Alex Thorne gripped her arm lightly and led her to the glowing fire. This time his hold on her didn't threaten broken bones. His strong fingers were just sufficiently persuasive to urge her along.

'While you're here, Erica,' he murmured, 'Mrs Roberts will fatten you up and bring a glow of health to your face.'

'I'm neither skinny nor weak!' Erica said sharply, longing to tear her arm from his grasp and march out of the room.

'Skinny? No,' he conceded, stopping to inspect her carefully. 'You're very slender, though. You're about half a stone underweight.' He glanced at her face which was flushed with annoyance. 'Good colour. You're probably healthy.'

She could see a devilish amusement dancing at the back of his eyes and Erica carefully removed her arm and stepped clear of him.

'Fortunately, you're not my doctor,' she reminded him sweetly. 'I've never been ill in my life.'

The words brought a slight cloud to her face and Erica looked rapidly away from the dark, probing gaze. Actually ill, no. But she had suffered, all the same. Traumatised was probably the right expression. Well, he didn't know about that, whatever his suspicions, and he was certainly not the sort of man she would confide in, however fraught things became.

Over dinner the words she had been dreading were spoken. She had managed to get this job by very skilful twisting and turning. On a stopover a few months ago she had arranged to meet her mother in London. Erica never went home now and meeting her mother at some designated place was the only way they could see each other. Rather than tell her mother the truth, Erica always pleaded pressure of work. There was not much time between one flight and another in any case and it was an easy subterfuge.

On this occasion she had persisted about her real father and finally her mother had told her the whole story. In the past, whenever she had brought up the subject she had been told only of her father's desertion. This time the truth had come out, and it had been no less painful that he had relentlessly gone his own way and left her mother alone, not knowing whether she was having a child or not. Not even caring, according to her mother's version.

Erica had thought of the distance to East Africa and told herself that the chance of ever going out there to confront him was very remote but this had been when her mother had mentioned a bit of information that had come her way.

'He's back in England,' she had said quietly. 'I saw it in the paper.'

'You mean he's famous?' Erica had looked at her in astonishment but her mother had shaken her head.

'No, he's not. It was a bit about the game reserve and the changes that are being made. It mentioned that the chief game warden was now in England and may not even go back. It was all about East Africa, a full-page spread, and this was just one bit of it. It said that Philip Macbride was in England and mentioned the man who had taken his place to continue his work.'

'So my name is really Macbride?' Erica said quietly, and her mother burst into her usual annoyance when the subject of Jack Linton was even vaguely mentioned.

'It's Linton! Jack made that legal when you were a baby and I don't know why you've come to be so hateful of him, Erica. I expect it's this stupid obsession with your father. Let me remind you that he never wanted to know you.'

'He didn't even know I was on the way to being born,' Erica countered, and her mother sniffed disdainfully.

'It wouldn't have made any difference. He followed his own path and anyone else was of no importance, including you, my girl. Just you remember that.'

Erica found the article in the library and read it avidly but, as her mother had said, there was just the vague mention of Philip Macbride. She pursued it all the same. She got in touch with the paper and told them she was doing a freelance article on him. They were wonderful and even ran him to earth for her. That didn't get her there, though. She had never had any intention of marching up and announcing herself.

Two flights later, her father played right into her hands all by himself. She was trying to save up to get a better flat and scanned every 'wanted' advertisement for some extra jobs she could do in her bit of spare time. Typing seemed an easy option because she had done a course at school and then taken a job in an office before she had joined the airline.

And there it was. 'Live-in secretary wanted for a month. Duties to type up the memoirs of a gentleman recently returned to England.' The name was Philip Macbride and the address was Keresford House, East Winton, Northumberland.

Erica applied at once, even before she had managed to get leave. She had to act fast and she could not risk anyone else getting the job. She wrote her own testimonials and prayed that he would not take up the references. He did not. Apparently, not many people fancied being up in Northumberland in November. He wrote back to her straight away and she had the job, just like that. It had been uncannily easy but now she had to face more than the pleased eyes of the man she had come to investigate.

There was Alex Thorne and he was intent on doing some investigations himself.

'Did you leave an important post to come here?' he asked casually as they sat in the dining room, which opened off the hall at the other side of the house.

'It wasn't important and I left a few weeks ago,' Erica said quickly. She had been prepared for some sort of question on those lines, and although it was difficult to lie to this dark-eyed man when she felt as if he could see right through her she didn't really have a lot of choice.

'You were bored with it?'

'In a way,' she agreed, her eyes remaining steadfastly on her food. 'I wanted to give myself time to look around a bit. I even considered working overseas but there was nothing in my line of work immediately available.'

'So this came at a very fortunate time?' he persisted, and Erica looked up and met his eyes fearlessly.

'Yes, it did. Just the sort of job I needed, the way I was feeling.'

'Lucky for me,' her father cut in. 'I'm not sure how long it will take to get everything sorted out and typed up. You'll be able to advise me on that, Erica. My notes are not exactly in good order.'

'Never mind,' she soothed, smiling at him. 'I like sorting things out.'

She needed to sort things out and not least her own mind. She had come here to spy on this man and then finally to confront him. She had come angrily and now she was very grateful that he was beside her. She was treating him as an ally, even as a saviour, someone to protect her against the persistence and cold probing of the man who sat across from her now and looked extremely sceptical about every word she uttered.

It was alarming to think that if she should be discovered there would not now be the calm option of turning round and blaming her father for his past crimes. Alex Thorne would be there and his reaction would not be calm at all.

Besides, she had never expected to find that her father was ill. It was not at all possible to take her original line now. And the worst thing was—she liked him. Philip Macbride was a gentle, generous man—just the sort of man she had needed all her life to stand by her and protect her. She had never had anyone to run to but she knew she would have been able to run to him. It gave her a very sad feeling, wiping out all her anger.

Erica's eyes strayed to the window. The long, heavy curtains had not been drawn across to shut out the night and snow hit the panes of glass like soft, enticing fingers, the feathery white crystals sliding down the warmer glass to lie in ever deepening layers against the edges of the panes.

'When this freezes, as it will later,' her father assured her, 'it will be cold enough to be dangerous out there. It's a long time since I was actually in England in the winter and I'm not really looking forward to it.'

'But it's beautiful all the same,' Erica murmured, her eyes still on the falling snow.

'Give me the sun any time,' her father muttered, and Erica silently agreed. There was a soft menace in the white beauty—a thing she had never thought before until she had found herself stranded this evening.

'You seem to have been in the sun not too long ago,' Alex said quietly, his eyes on Erica's lightly tanned skin. She had. Her last stopover in Singapore had been for longer than usual and she had rushed to the hotel pool and soaked up the sun.

'I'm just this colour,' she assured him hastily, avoiding his eyes by eating her meal. 'Some people are.'

'But few redheads. With your colouring you should take care in the sun.'

'I rarely get the chance to be in it,' Erica countered firmly. 'There's not much sun in an office.'

'And not much danger,' Alex replied. She looked up and found his eyes on her face, and a very thoughtful expression came into them as they held her own gaze effortlessly. 'Never mind,' he assured her softly. 'You're quite safe here.'

His glance told her otherwise and there was much more menace in his tone than in the soft white threat of the snow outside.

CHAPTER THREE

NEXT day, as she had expected, Erica looked out of her bedroom window to find that the house was surrounded by deep snow. The sun was shining but it was having no effect whatever on the frozen expanse of white. The trees were really beautiful, each branch hung with heavy, glittering white, and she could have stayed there for ages just looking at the scene, but instead she hurried to get ready. Today was the day she started to work for her father and she hoped she could manage it and still remember her office skills.

She was terribly nervous. Thinking about it in London had not prepared her for the actual deceit. She would be facing her father every day and, while she had the feeling that he would neither know nor care if she was a bit rusty with her typing, there was somebody else who would care and he would spot her for a fraud without much investigation.

Her initial meeting with Alex Thorne had antagonised him but she knew for sure that even if he had just come home to find her already here he would not have been any different. He was clever and he seemed to have suspected her even when he was typing the letter offering her the post here.

She dressed in soft green woollen trousers and a matching sweater and went down to see what was happening. She had slept very well in spite of her nervous misgivings and this morning she felt much more sure of herself, though still not up to facing Alex Thorne.

'I've put you in the little breakfast room, dear,' Mrs Roberts told her as she came down into the hall. 'Mr Macbride and the doctor have eaten already.'

'Am I late?' Erica asked, immediately anxious, but Mrs Roberts gave her a smile of reassurance.

'Good heavens, no! It's only half past eight. It's just that Mr Macbride is used to getting up early. I expect it's up with the sun in Africa with all those animals to see to.'

She said it as though he had been accustomed to feeding all the animals on the game reserve by hand and Erica found her lips twitching in amusement.

'Is Dr Thorne out?' she asked, her amusement dying at the thought that he might suddenly appear and pounce on her.

'Only in the park,' Mrs Roberts informed her. 'We're snowed in at the moment but they'll be up here quickly to make sure the doctor can get to the main road. He has to be at the hospital by ten. No, at the moment he's out with the dog. Charlie insists on his walk whatever the weather decides to do.'

She showed Erica to the breakfast room and hurried off to bring her meal, and Erica sat at the table and looked out across the grounds. This was another side of the house and in the summer this room would be flooded by sunlight. It was very bright now in fact. The sun hit the snow, dazzling the eye and making the room seem extraordinarily light.

There were fields and trees for as far as she could see and she wondered if they belonged to the house. It was certainly a beautiful place to live. She had not really given much thought to the sort of house she would be coming to. Her only concern had been to get to her father and watch him. This place, though, made her feel even more of an intruder, out of her depth, and she knew she would have to struggle with the feeling if she stayed.

As she was eating her breakfast she still found her eyes contemplating the scenery, and as she watched she saw Charlie leaping about in the snow with more energy than she would have thought possible after his reluctance to move last night.

He was delighted with himself, stopping every couple of yards to roll in the crisp snow, until his black coat was white all over. She heard a sharp whistle and Charlie went bounding off to appear a few seconds later frisking along at the heels of the man who scared Erica more than a little.

Alex Thorne was dressed for the weather, wearing a heavy white high-necked sweater under a dark weatherproof jacket. His strong legs were encased in dark trousers and he had on some sort of walking boots, thick socks turned over the tops.

Erica frowned. He looked disgustingly healthy. He was tramping through the deep snow with his hands in the pockets of his jacket, his black hair contrasting with the snow as much as Charlie's coat did. He was coming back, too, and she hastily got on with her breakfast, trying to calculate how long it would take him to get here and if Mrs Roberts would be offended if she simply left the rest and rushed off.

It would have made no difference. He vaulted over the fence and came across the snow towards her side of the house, obviously intending to come in by the back door. Erica hoped he would then go to get changed and give her time to escape. The sight of him brought all her misgivings back with a rush.

But he'd seen her in any case. He raised his hand in greeting and a wide grin spread across his face as Erica gave him a very small, brittle smile. That was it. She gulped down her tea and fled from the room. If he was coming in for a hot drink he could have one in solitary splendour.

The trouble was that she didn't know where to go, and she came to a halt in the hall, hoping to see Mrs Roberts and get directions before Alex Thorne came through. Luck, apparently, was against her because he appeared right then. His jacket had been discarded and so had the boots and he was standing there, six feet two literally in socks, the same wry grin tilting his lips.

'Ready for action?' he enquired quizzically when Erica just stood and looked at him bleakly. 'It takes Philip a good while to wind up in the morning these days but with any luck he'll be in his little study. I hope it's going to be big enough for both of you because you certainly can't have mine.'

He came padding forward silently, clearly intent on showing her the way, and Erica had to force herself not to back away. He looked like one of the big cats, menacingly tranquil, and she burst into nervous speech.

'I wonder what became of my car?' she said hurriedly. 'I intended to ring someone up last night and make arrangements for it to be collected. I forgot, I'm afraid.'

'I didn't forget,' he assured her quietly. 'I made all the arrangements while you were getting ready for dinner. They should have it back here complete with new tyre and new spare tyre by the time the road is cleared.'

'That was very kind of you,' Erica murmured, quite astounded at this Good Samaritan attitude.

'Was it?' He stopped and looked down at her with taunting astonishment, his hand on a door that she assumed led to her father's study. 'It must have been an oversight. I'll try not to let it happen again.'

'You and I are not going to get on well at all, are we, Dr Thorne?' Erica said a trifle bitterly, once again feeling that she had taken a minor beating.

'Time will tell,' he murmured, still standing with his hand on the closed door and blocking her way through. 'When I've got you sorted out we'll consider the position further.'

'It doesn't really matter, Dr Thorne,' Erica assured him in a sharp little voice. 'I'm working for Mr Macbride. It's just unfortunate that I'm also obliged to be in your house.'

He stared at her disconcertingly but this time she refused to back down and look away. She didn't even care if she had been rude.

'It's unfortunate,' he agreed softly. He suddenly lifted his hand and tilted her face with firm fingers. 'You're a beautiful little thing, Erica Linton, but there's something about you that doesn't quite ring true. When I know what it is, I'll be more easy in my mind.'

'You imagine I'm here to murder your stepfather?' Erica raged in a low voice, well aware that her father might be at the other side of the door.

'Not really,' he mused, tightening his grip on her chin when she attempted to move away. 'As I said last night, you're about half a stone underweight.' He suddenly smiled into her eyes, his lips twisting in amusement, laughter bubbling just below the surface. 'No, I don't fear for his safety as far as you're concerned. It's not that at all. Maybe it's your edginess.'

'You're causing that, Dr Thorne!' Erica snapped, irritated beyond words that he still held her face tilted as if she were a child having to face a sardonic schoolmaster.

He actually laughed aloud then and let her go, but before she had escaped entirely he said her name softly and had her turning back to him.

'Erica,' he warned, 'he's a sick man at the moment. Watch him. I can't be here all the time and he never knows when to stop. I'm relying on you to stop him when he looks exhausted, or even before then.'

'How can I?' she pleaded, her blue eyes puzzled and enormous as she tried to reckon up this swift change of attitude. 'I'm working here. I have to do as I'm told.'

'That should be worth seeing,' he murmured, his eyes highly amused. 'However, you can threaten him with me.'

'I've not been here long enough,' she pointed out, and he cocked his head on one side and looked at her levelly.

'I'm thinking about the long days of the future,' he explained. 'Philip will become enthusiastic. This book is as close as he's going to get to his beloved animals for some considerable time. He seems to like you and I have a definite feeling that you like him. Two enthusiastic people enclosed in this study will mean too much work for Philip. Watch him.'

'Very well, Dr Thorne,' Erica said in her most formal voice. 'I'll do my best.'

'I'm sure you will, Erica.' Then he warned softly, 'If you don't, I'll hold you responsible.'

Erica turned away angrily and was brought to an abrupt halt, her eyes wide with shock as he wound his hand swiftly in her hair and gave it a sharp tug.

'Call me Alex,' he suggested. 'It's more homely.'

'How—how dare you...?' Erica began, her hand coming to the smarting place on her head where his sharp tug had left its mark.

'Easily,' he assured her silkily. 'I'm beginning to think of you as a wayward child—but devious, Erica, very devious.'

He just walked off, and Erica had to take quite a few deep breaths before she could calm down enough to knock on the door and go inside to face her father.

He was sitting there rummaging through the papers on his desk and she thought wryly that her first job would be to sort this lot out. He seemed to be drowning in papers and from the way he was handling them it seemed that he didn't much care where they fell when they left his hand.

'Erica,' he stated mournfully, 'this is not going to work. You'll never be able to read my writing. It's something I didn't even think of when I placed the advertisement.'

Last night, before she had met him and talked to him, Erica would have seized the chance and said, Never mind. No harm done, and left there and then. Instead she found herself smiling as she came to the desk and was somewhat astonished to hear her voice soothing him.

'I'll soon get to know your little quirks of writing,' she said quietly. 'I think it might be an idea if I sorted this lot out to begin with.'

'Well, the pages are numbered,' he told her quite proudly. 'That should help.'

'No problem,' she assured him. 'Shall I work over here?'

It was a small room but not the tiny little place that Alex had led her to expect. She frowned at her thoughts. Alex? She had no intention of calling him anything of the sort. She wasn't even going to think the name.

There was another desk by the window and she settled down there with the papers, quite pleased that she could look out and see the lovely scenery as she worked. This house was a very tranquil place, which was surprising when you considered the sort of man who owned it. He wasn't her idea of a doctor. She wondered if he had a practice in the village or if he had patients coming to the house.

'Will we manage in this little room, do you think?' her father asked, and she looked up with a bright smile.

'Of course! We're not likely to want to run about, are we? And I'm going to love working here by the window.'

'Alex came up with that electric typewriter,' Philip pointed out. 'I hope it's all right. He said you may want a word processor.'

'This is fine,' she assured him hastily.

Word processor! Perish the thought. It would be some time before she made any speed on the typewriter and she had never used a word processor in her life. It was another oversight and if the suspicious doctor mentioned it she would just have to say that she was prepared to manage with what she had right here. What she would do if he came in carrying one of the dreaded machines she just didn't know. He would probably be prepared to go to any sort of expense to trap her.

She heard the sound of a snowplough a little later and one actually came roaring up the drive. They certainly intended that the doctor wouldn't be trapped here all day. Erica wondered if all doctors got this gilt-edged treatment. She doubted it.

After a while, the Mercedes came slowly round to the front of the house and Alex Thorne got out and went indoors. He was still in his thick clothes and she assumed that he had been getting the snow off the car because the windscreen and the sides had been recently cleared. He came back out in about twenty minutes and she had to stop what she was doing to watch him.

He looked totally different and Erica felt a wave of dismay. He looked devastating. He was in a dark blue suit and crisp white shirt and she had visions of hoards of underlings following him across a ward, all hanging onto his every word. He wasn't going to open up a village surgery looking like that and she remembered that Mrs Roberts had said he had to be at the hospital at ten. What did he do? Had she actually set about somebody who was very important? The idea dashed any feeling of tranquillity and she just stared miserably out of the window.

He was completely unsmiling, not at all like the man who had been playing with the dog earlier. He looked as if he had a lot on his mind and it was clear that the house and anyone in it had now been banished from his thoughts. He looked handsome too. Of course she had noticed that before, but now his good looks and dark colouring seemed to leap out and hit her.

He tossed a leather case into the back seat and then got into his car and moved off down the newly cleared drive. She just stared after him, puzzled that his obvious importance had left her feeling deflated.

'Oh, Alex is going.' Her father glanced at his watch and then looked back through the window. 'He'll be a bit late today. They'll all be waiting.'

'A—a lot of patients?' Erica asked uneasily.

'And students,' he said. 'He's a consultant at the hospital.'

'Then—then I shouldn't have been calling him Doctor. It's Mr Thorne.'

'No. He's not a surgeon. Surgeons are mister but physicians are doctor. Some obscure etiquette. It's all a mystery to me.'

Erica still watched the car. She noted that it was a *new* Mercedes. It was more than a mystery to her. How had she ever become entangled in this splendid household and how did she imagine she would get away with it? She was just an ordinary girl from the suburbs who wore a uniform for work and did a tiring job that was not as glamorous as it seemed to outsiders.

While she was dishing up meals to uneasy travellers, fetching them drinks and seeing to their needs, Alex Thorne was making grave decisions, comforting very sick people. She often thought of herself as being merely a flying waitress, and he was an important man. What nasty trick of fate had stranded her in the snow and allowed her to rage at him? Still, she was quite used to nasty tricks of fate.

Her father was busily writing again and Erica sorted out the papers without too much trouble. She had not attempted to read anything because one glance at the writing had assured her that she would have to learn it like tackling a new language. This was going to take longer than she had anticipated and now that she had seen the volume of work and the difficulty a month seemed to be a very short time.

She glanced at her father and then found her eyes lingering on him. It was impossible to believe that a man like this would walk out and shelve his responsibilities. He looked gentle, kind and there was something about him that made her think he would be devoted to any cause he took up. Maybe that was it. Maybe he had been so devoted to his work that he had been prepared to leave her mother and just walk off.

Erica decided to read for a while and then start as soon as she could reasonably decipher the words. She had to read the first few pages more than once, filling in the words she could not fathom by making a guess or two, but gradually she began to get used to the wildly sprawling hand and the indifferently formed letters. She sank into the reading and it was fascinating.

'Are you managing?'

She looked up to find her father watching her and she realised that quite a long time had passed and she had simply been reading avidly.

'I've got the hang of it,' she told him quickly, and then she could not stop the smile that came to her face. 'It's enthralling. I won't be able to type for reading it.'

'Do you think so, Erica?' he asked eagerly. 'You're the first person to get a look at it. I wondered at one time if I was just being foolish in doing this book.'

'Oh, no! It's wonderful,' Erica assured him. 'It's flashing before my eyes like a film. Are you going to illustrate it with photographs?'

'A few. Mostly they'll be sketches. I'll get them out this afternoon and show you. I'd like your opinion on those too. I'm used to sketching animals and making notes but I don't know if they're professional enough.'

'I'll start typing,' Erica stated firmly. 'It will take me a while to work into it.'

'Not surprising with my handwriting,' he muttered, and she felt a great wave of relief. There was her excuse, ready-made. By the time she had worked up some speed, Alex Thorne would have forgotten all his suspicions.

'Don't work too hard,' she warned, remembering the orders that had been given to her this morning, and her father glanced across at her with a wry grin.

'Been getting at you, has he? Mrs Roberts spies on me too. I'm only safe in here and now Alex's actually got a spy into my study.'

'I'll report nothing,' Erica said firmly. 'Remember, though, that if you're ill the work will have to stop. It's better to go along easily than wear yourself out. But you can forget about me spying. If Dr Thorne wants to know anything then he'll just have to ask Mrs Roberts.'

'You and I are going to get on very well indeed, Erica,' her father chuckled, 'and, just for you, I'll take it nice and easy.'

Erica nodded and started to type. Mission accomplished. Getting him to slow down would be no problem. She would talk at him if he seemed to be going too hard. Jeremy often said that she talked at people and not to them. It might be a useful skill in this case. She felt a twinge of anxiety at the thought of Jeremy. She must get in touch with him. He had to keep right out of her life until this whole thing was over. She wanted no more complications.

In the afternoon, her car was delivered and she also found that it had been paid for. That put her in a very awkward position and Erica decided that as soon as Alex came home she would tackle him. She wasn't going to wait until he told her how much she owed him. Her immediate plans were frustrated, however, when Mrs Roberts came into her father's study in the late afternoon and announced that Dr Thorne would not be home for dinner.

'He's got an emergency,' she announced solemnly. 'He's had to turn round and go back to the hospital. Some poor soul. Still, Dr Thorne is used to it, I suppose, but I must say I could never cope with other people's suffering.' She nodded at both of them very gravely and went out and Philip Macbride shook his head in exasperation.

'Mrs Roberts can be very depressing when she gets started on the subject of health. I'd rather have you as a spy any day, Erica.'

'I'm not a spy,' Erica assured him, but when he had turned back to his papers she bit uneasily at her lip.

What was she doing here but spying on him, after all? She had come here for that purpose alone. She had come to look him over and then devastate him with her knowledge. That was spying of the worst kind and she knew that now she could never do it. He was a nice man and he was ill. There was no way she could carry out her original intentions.

Dinnertime came and went and still Alex did not come home. The snow had started again as soon as darkness had fallen and Erica found to her extreme annoyance that she was watching the drive rather anxiously, waiting to see the lights of the Mercedes, wondering if driving conditions were dangerous.

She got a firm grip on herself and went up to her room. What did she care if he was out in a blizzard? It must be Mrs Roberts' glum outlook that had unsettled her. She went back downstairs later and popped her head into the study, greatly pleased to see that her father was not working on. When she peeped into the rather cosy little room that was at the side of the grander drawing room, she found him watching television, and she really felt then that her duties for the day were over.

She closed the door quietly and was just on her way back across the hall when the front door opened and Alex came in. He still looked immaculate but he looked very tired and she stopped and stared at him, astonished to see an odd sort of vulnerability in his face.

'Erica.' He just nodded at her and set off for the stairs and she forgot all about her car.

'Shall I tell Mrs Roberts you're here?' she asked. 'We had dinner ages ago. Shall I tell her to get yours now?'

'No, thanks. I ate at the hospital. She can get off to her little cottage. The snow is back with a vengeance.'

He gave her a rather grim smile and continued on his way but Erica couldn't seem to stop watching him and he noticed.

'Something wrong?' He turned to look at her but she shook her head vigorously.

'No, nothing. Mr Macbride didn't work too hard and we got started. I can even read his writing . . .' Her voice tailed away and she looked embarrassed. She was talking at him. She was doing it nervously too. 'You look tired,' she blurted out. 'Should I get you a cup of tea?'

'No, you shouldn't, Erica.' A slight smile touched his lips. 'You seem to have carried out my orders. Don't get nervous because I'm in my working uniform. I'm not about to prescribe some hideous medicine and make you take it.'

He seemed to have no difficulty in picking up her vibes at any time and she supposed that it was his training. It must be like being a sort of medical detective to work at his level. No wonder he had that probing look about him. Maybe he was like that with everybody.

'Can I go now?' he asked in amusement when she just stood gazing at him, and she felt her face flushing hotly.

'I'm sorry,' she muttered. 'I didn't mean to keep you talking.'

'It's quite cheered me up,' he assured her softly. 'It must be something about you. You tend to take my mind off other things.'

Which meant that his mind was now back on her possibly devious actions. She had meant to go upstairs but that was where he was going and Erica scuttled off to the study, glancing at him surreptitiously as she got to the door. He was walking up the stairs, a half-smile on his face, and she wondered just what he was thinking. It would always be impossible to tell.

A little while later she ventured out of her hiding place and went up to her room. She didn't quite know where else to go because she had not been here long enough to fit into the household in any way. To go into the little room where her father was watching television would be intruding; in fact she felt she would be intruding wherever she went so her own room seemed to be the safest bet.

Before she had managed it, she almost bumped head-on into Alex who was just coming along the passage upstairs.

'Poor little thing,' he murmured ironically. 'Nowhere to go. Follow me.' His hand clamped round her wrist and Erica found herself being turned back towards the stairs.

'I was going to my room,' she protested, but she didn't quite have the nerve to jerk her wrist from the deceptively casual grasp.

'You were going there because you couldn't think of any other place to go. This state of affairs must be corrected. You are now living in my house.'

'I'm just a temporary secretary,' Erica pointed out, trying to drag her heels without its being obvious. 'I'm not a guest.'

He stopped and looked down at her, still keeping the restraining hand in position. He had changed into casual clothes and now he didn't look quite so formidable but the memory of it still lingered in her mind.

'You're here for quite a while. I can't have you lurking in corners, hiding your head. You can't watch Philip if you're locked in your room.'

'But you're here now! I've watched him all day.'

'I'm tired. You said so yourself. You even tried to make me drink tea. In any case, Philip takes a lot of watching and I have to train you. Actually,' he conceded, 'I'm quite pleased with you. There's a streak of kindness in you, in spite of your ability to rage madly.'

'I do not like being laughed at,' Erica told him sharply. 'And I do not like being treated as if I were a child. I'm working for your stepfather and for the rest of the time if I want to creep about and hide I will do so.'

'It's *why* you are hiding that intrigues me,' Alex informed her quietly. 'Almost every word you say is a little barrier to conceal something.'

'Stop prying into my head!' she ordered angrily, glaring at him.

'It's a habit of mine. I'm not capable of stopping. If I stopped, I wouldn't be able to do my job. Let's continue, shall we?'

He set off again and Erica didn't know whether to scream at him or burst into hysterical laughter. He just didn't behave like other people and he had a familiar way of treating her, as if she had known him for years. It must be because of their unusual meeting. That thought brought another one and she stopped at the top of the stairs and looked up at him stubbornly.

'How much do I owe you for my car repairs?' she asked crisply.

'Ten thousand pounds,' he said blandly, and she pulled free of him and looked at him furiously.

'Can't you be serious?' she blazed, and he looked at her for a minute, all humour dying on his face.

'I've been serious all day. I'll be serious tomorrow because the same problem will still be there. Sometimes, I can't quite shake it off. Entertain me, Erica. I need it.'

The usual sarcastic words refused to spring to her lips and she looked at him with sympathy in her eyes even though she was telling herself that she didn't care how hard his day had been.

'I'm sorry if you've had a bad day,' she said quietly. 'Just tell me what I owe you, Dr Thorne, and I'll not pester you again.'

'I'll tell you if you promise to call me Alex in future,' he offered, and Erica found her lips quirking in spite of her misgivings.

'All right. If you want a lack of formality I can't really refuse. You're the boss.'

'I'm glad you noticed,' he said quietly. 'Now come downstairs and I'll show you where you can watch television and get yourself a drink if you want one, and then you can look in the kitchen and even make yourself some tea.'

Erica sighed and went along with him. She didn't seem to have a lot of choice and her father actually appeared glad to see her when they went into the little room. She noticed that he never once mentioned Alex's bad day; apparently it was a subject that was not to be broached.

'Let's have that tea, shall we?' Alex sat down and looked up at her and Erica had no alternative. She went along to the kitchen and made a tray up for three. If she was going to be forced into acting like a member of this household then she might as well enjoy it.

She was more or less trapped into watching the news on television and when it was over she collected the tea things and went to wash them up in the kitchen. She didn't miss Alex's amused look either, but she wasn't very concerned. Sooner or later she would have to find a niche for herself in this house and tonight had at least been a start.

The snow still fell heavily and when she was in bed with the lights out Erica could hear the wind whining round the house, whistling by the tall chimney pots, and she could just imagine that tomorrow the snowplough would have to come back and let Alex out again. If someone was very ill he would want to be off early.

She fell asleep thinking about his strange ways. She had never met anyone like him before and she wished she had not come here under false pretences. She wished she had just been here as a guest, visiting her father. She dared not even begin to think how angry Alex would be if he ever discovered that he had a stepsister—a very devious stepsister who worked in the house at the side of her father and said nothing at all to let them know the truth. He would never find out because as soon as she reasonably could she would leave here and go back to London and her real job.

Coming here had been a bad mistake but at least she had made her mind up about one thing: she could never imagine Philip Macbride abandoning anyone.

He had not known that he was to be a father. Any other troubles were none of her business. Some people found it impossible to get on with each other and a kind, imaginative man with a great love of Africa and the wildlife there would not have very much in common with her mother. It was really nothing to do with her. She had found out all she wanted to know and she would never let him learn that he had left a daughter behind. It would hurt him unnecessarily.

CHAPTER FOUR

WITH her place in the household fairly well fixed, Erica soon fell into a routine. After breakfast each day she worked with her father and he seemed to be keeping his promise to take it easy. It was exciting—much more absorbing than she had expected it to be. As the book grew under her hands, the life he had led in East Africa unfolded. He wrote in a very down-to-earth, racy style that was easy to read and amusing and her father often raised his head with a pleased smile when she failed to suppress a chuckle at some of his remarks.

The sketches he had made were beautiful, fine line-drawings in ink that expressed the movement and moods of the animals. One or two he had put aside as not really suitable although Erica could not see why. It was these few, though, that gave her an idea and as the week went by the idea grew into an enthusiastic need for action on the subject.

When her car had been delivered, the tyre had already been repaired and the wheel inspected for damage. Luckily she had driven slowly and carefully after the tyre had collapsed and there had been no damage to the actual wheel. On opening the boot she had found also that the spare was no longer the liability it had been. She was legal again. The car was ready for the road.

If she had been in her original mood she would have left, but things had changed. She was becoming more fond of her father with each passing day and she could not even consider upsetting him. If she simply left he

would be puzzled and disappointed. It would stay on her
conscience for the rest of her life and she would never
see him again.

She had hardly seen Alex at all but when she had seen
him he had looked tired and strained. He was rarely in
for dinner and she assumed that things were not going
too well with one or more patients.

'He takes it too much to heart,' Mrs Roberts confided
gloomily. 'If they don't get better quickly he's under
stress. He fights for them too hard. He can't afford to
be like that. He should really keep aloof. In his position
he can't be fretting over every patient who's not re-
sponding to treatment.'

Erica looked at her askance. If *she* had been ill she
would have liked to know that the man in charge was
concerned enough to be anxious. Mrs Roberts seemed
to think that Alex should stay on some cloud of importance and never step down from it.

'I would think he has his own way of working,' she
pointed out firmly, surprised that she felt a need to
defend him.

'Takes it right to heart and takes on too much.' Mrs
Roberts sniffed. 'No need to do this accident-emergency
thing either. That's for ordinary doctors.'

'Perhaps he feels ordinary,' Erica murmured, backing
out of the kitchen and wishing she had never offered to
get a cup of tea for her father.

'No use wishing for the impossible. He can't be ordinary, not with his skills.' She turned to Erica with a
look of fervour. 'They come from far and wide to see
him. Some people are sent from London and he lectures
there. They even come from America,' she added in an
awed voice. 'There's nobody to touch Dr Thorne. He
shouldn't be in a northern hospital, away from it all.'

'He lives here,' Erica reminded her, thankfully making it to the door.

'Shouldn't do. Should be in the middle of things. Still, if he left here, he wouldn't have me. I couldn't move south.'

'There you are, then,' Erica proclaimed, diving through the door with the tea-tray and breathing a sigh of relief as she heard it close behind her. She knew now why her father tried to keep Mrs Roberts off the subject of health. It was some sort of obsession. At other times she was homely and normal.

Erica was grinning as she went into the study and her father wanted to know why.

'It takes all sorts,' he muttered as she acquainted him with the facts. 'I'm glad she's not a nurse. Mind you,' he added quietly, 'in a way, it's true. Alex could go just about anywhere. I've never met anyone quite like him. We were hoping he would come back to Africa and work there but he did all his studying in England. His father left him this house and plenty of money and I suppose the north is in his blood just as Africa is in mine. He just stayed on here. It all boils down to roots, I expect.'

Erica nodded and got on with her work. She didn't seem to have any roots. She had never been comfortable enough at home to dare put down any roots and her job meant that she was never in one place long enough to really settle. It was hard to feel that a flat in London was home, and in any case she was never in it for very long. It was pretty dismal too.

She pulled herself together and got on rapidly. There was little point in thinking of what might have been. Even if her father had known of her existence he would probably still have felt too strongly about Africa to stay and take care of her. That would have been left to her mother, and though there would never have been any Jack Linton things would have been bleak.

'Can I keep these drawings that you're going to discard?' she asked her father at lunchtime, and he looked extremely honoured.

'If you think they're worth keeping, Erica,' he agreed. 'There's something wrong with them. They look a bit flat to me.' And Erica knew exactly why. That was the cause of her bubbling excitement.

After lunch she always had a spare hour and today she intended to use it to make a trip to the village. She got a few anxious warnings from her father when she announced this but she smiled at his worries.

'The snowplough keeps things clear,' she pointed out. 'Apart from the drive it's all on the one road. I'll not be long.' She stopped at the door and looked at him seriously. 'You'll take your little rest, won't you?'

'I promised and I will.' He gave a chuckle and looked up at her with a very mischievous grin. 'I don't mind doing it for you, Erica. Mrs Roberts points things out in an entirely different way. I'm afraid I delight in disobeying her.'

Erica shook her head and gave him a severe frown but she couldn't keep the smile from her face. She seemed to be getting on with him so very well that sometimes it was difficult to believe that he didn't know who she was.

She set off for the village, her first trip out since she had come here with Alex. The snow was banked high at the sides of the road, pushed there on the many trips made by the snowploughs, and there was a quite cruel wind whistling across the open fields. It was warm in her car but even at lunchtime she would not have liked to be out walking in this icy cold. It was so different from London. When night came it would be pitilessly harsh, not the sort of place to be stranded or out on foot.

She wished now that she had brought more practical clothes with her. She had enough warm things to wear but she had not really envisaged this sort of weather and she would have felt more secure if she had been wearing thicker trousers and some sort of heavy boots. Not that she intended walking, but there was a primitive feeling about the weather that alerted her basic instinct for survival.

Erica stopped by the post office and hurried inside. She might just get what she wanted here. The place seemed to be a general store and looked as if it kept anything the people in the village would want. It did not, however, have watercolour paints and Erica felt quite foolish when she asked.

'Just the little tins of paint that children buy for their colouring books would do,' she murmured when the man behind the counter looked at her in blank astonishment.

'We don't get things like that in until Christmas,' he said, adding after giving it some more thought, 'The only other shops here are the butcher's and the bread shop. They'll not sell paints, mind you.'

Erica hadn't imagined that they would. She nodded glumly and walked to the door. It had dashed her enthusiasm. She would have been able to get anything she wanted in London and the thought of being thwarted in her plans was annoying.

'There's a craft shop,' the man added as she opened the door to the icy wind outside. 'They'll not be open in this season. They only open for tourists in summer, but they live at the place and they're probably in now. It's a cottage down the lane. Maybe they would sell paints, not that I know.'

'Where is it?' Erica asked eagerly, enthusiasm returning with a joyful bound.

'There's a little road off by the church.' He looked dubiously at her boots. 'You'll have to walk, though. The plough doesn't get down there.'

'Is it far?' Erica asked, determined not to be put off even if it was freezing outside.

'Couple of hundred yards,' he assured her, coming to the door. He pointed to the church further down the street. 'You can park on the road there and walk down the lane to it. Few minutes' walk.'

She nodded her thanks and went back to her car. The street was icing up but she stuck stubbornly to her mission. A few minutes' walk and she would have what she wanted. It would mean she had something to do in the evenings, and in any case she was almost childishly eager to carry out her plan and show the results to her father.

She would have to stop thinking of him like that, she remonstrated with herself. She should think of him as Mr Macbride; after all, she called him that. If she went on like this she was going to miss him when she left and she intended to leave as soon as it was feasible. She would not let him down but when the typing was done she would have to go.

Erica frowned to herself. She had taken to thinking of Alex Thorne by his first name too. She managed to avoid using it when she spoke to him but she thought of him as Alex and that was not a good idea either. He was nothing to her and she would be gone soon and never even think of him again. She pulled up by the church and got out. Even beginning the walk was not easy because she had to climb over the banked snow.

Whoever lived at the craft cottage had not been out so far.

Ten cold minutes later she stopped and took stock of her surroundings, wondering if the man at the village shop was a sadist. She had been ploughing through fairly deep snow since she had parked her car by the church and so far she had seen no sign at all of a cottage of any sort, craft shop or otherwise.

Since she had passed the gates to the church there had been nothing but snow-covered trees and hedges. There wasn't even a vicarage. It must be the right lane because there had been no other lane at all by the church. She looked at her watch and decided to go for another five minutes and then give up the search. Going back up the lane, she would be facing into the icy wind and the going would be even more uncomfortable.

It *was* more uncomfortable; in fact, that was putting it very mildly. Erica was glad she had given herself a time limit because when she turned around and faced a fifteen-minute walk back to her car she knew she had been particularly foolish as it was. And there had been no sign of any cottage. It had all been wasted effort.

The snow was beginning again, not the fat, deceptively beautiful flakes she had watched from the warmth and comfort of the house but icy particles that stung her already reddened cheeks and made her pull the hood of her white jacket round her face. The hood was edged with fur but it was completely useless as a foil for the bitter cold. The dark fur might look pretty against her red hair and glowing cheeks but she was already shivering in spite of her forced exercise.

The wind whistled through her, pointing out to her the unsuitability of thin, woollen trousers, and her boots were soaked with the wet, stained and darkened by the snow. She knew she would have been better off in wellington boots but, unfortunately, she didn't possess any.

Erica put her head down and trudged on, falling two or three times on the rather slippery track and getting more wet and cold in the process. She was so busy watching her feet and forcing her mind to reject the cold that she came to a stop in quite a state of shock when her downward gaze encountered two booted feet with strong legs attached and the edge of a thick, sheepskin jacket.

Erica looked up and her startled gaze encountered Alex's dark-eyed stare of frustration.

'You never mentioned insanity in that wonderful letter you sent to Philip,' he grated. 'What the devil are you doing now?'

'You're home early.' Erica stood clutching her hood around her face, very grateful that his powerful frame was blocking out the driving sleet.

'Which is probably just as well,' he snapped, grabbing her arm and turning her towards the village. 'I saw your car and my heart almost stopped beating. I knew it was going to be another bad day. You're a mobile disaster area!'

'I just came out for a while,' Erica muttered defensively. 'I had some shopping to do.'

'Really? Frozen turnips?' he rasped sarcastically. 'What did you expect to find down that lane, a beauty parlour?'

'I was looking for a craft shop,' Erica managed huffily. He was striding along like a giant and she was sliding about all over the place. If he had let her arm go free she would have fallen flat on her face.

'I suppose you mean the cottage,' he muttered. 'You passed it. It's just around the back of the church, up a little track.'

'The man at the shop never said that,' Erica protested hotly, and he gave a grunt of further exasperation.

'Knowing you, you probably rushed off before he could complete his directions. Things move slowly in these parts.'

'Including minds,' Erica put in sharply. 'He actually came to the door and pointed. He said the cottage was a couple of hundred yards up the lane.'

'And do you know how far a couple of hundred yards is, Erica?' Alex asked with irritated patience, turning her to face him as they finally got back to the cars.

'I—I walked for fifteen minutes before I turned back,' she confessed, and the dark brows rose in sardonic astonishment.

'I'll take some time off soon and give you a few lessons in measuring,' he promised wryly. He glanced down at her shivering form. 'Haven't you got any real clothes?' he grated, annoyance rushing back at the sight of her cold, wet appearance.

'All my clothes are real.' Erica glared up at him, ignoring the icy lash of the sleet.

'For a cool day in London,' he agreed irascibly. 'Here, you need thick boots, woollen socks, heavy trousers and sweaters. You probably need thermal undies.'

'You have no right to speak like that!' Erica gasped, her cheeks redder than ever.

'Don't be so damned naïve!' he snapped. 'Your fashionable clothes are not concealing anything I haven't seen before.'

'You—you're a doctor!' Erica said, outraged and embarrassed. 'You therefore have no business to be speaking like that.'

'When I look at you,' he growled, 'I'm nothing but a very exasperated male. What I do for a living never enters my mind. Get in your car and drive off in front of me,' he ordered furiously. 'That way I'll be able to see you all the time and save myself the trouble of coming back for you when you run off the road into a tree.'

Erica turned away, her face flaming and her temper on the edge of boiling over. He grasped her arm again and spun her round.

'What did you want a craft shop for?' he asked, frowning at her ferociously.

'I wanted some watercolours.' Erica threw back her head and looked at him haughtily. 'I want to paint. I do have free time, you know, and I wanted something to do with it. I'm not used to simply hanging around.'

'I can believe that,' he muttered. 'I'm amazed that the house has been able to contain you so far. Philip must have more charm than he realises. You look very much like a "here today and gone tomorrow" person to me.'

'All right! I'll *go* tomorrow!' Erica shouted. Her hood had fallen down now and she stood there in a fury, her dark red hair flying round her face, her dark blue eyes almost black with rage.

'No, you won't,' he growled. 'You're doing Philip a lot of good. You may infuriate me but you certainly soothe him. If you try to leave, I'll tie you to the desk.'

'Well—well, just leave me alone, then,' Erica managed, surprised and delighted at this admission that she was good for her father.

'How can I leave you alone?' he asked quietly, his temper dying away as the dark eyes scanned her heated face. 'I have to fathom you out. I have to find out why you're here.'

'To help my—employer.' Erica stared at him in horror. She had almost said 'father' and his eyes narrowed alarmingly at her hesitation over the word.

'Very formal,' he murmured. 'You're here for more than that, Erica. I've been very busy since you came. I have two patients battling with a great deal of pain but they'll recover, and when they do I'll turn my attention to you.' He looked at her with open disapproval. 'Now get into that car and set off. If you catch a chill it will be Mrs Roberts looking after you. I save my time for the deserving sick, not for idiotic girls who dash out into the bitter cold on mad sprees.'

Erica turned away angrily, opening her car door, determined not to look at him again. The next time Mrs Roberts gave a critical lecture about his ways she would keep quiet and nod her approval.

'What are you going to paint?'

Apparently he had been mulling it over, and as far as Erica was concerned he could go on mulling.

'I'm not telling you!' she informed him angrily, and she heard his low mutter of annoyance as she got into her car and set off.

She was soaking wet and her boots were ruined. She was sticking to the seat of the car because when she had fallen her trousers had become wet too. Her face tightened with annoyance when she remembered his remarks about thermal undies. He was too familiar. She had often tried to work out why he got under her skin and now it was very clear why. He had treated her in this familiar manner since she had come here. Maybe he thought that being a consultant of staggering importance gave him the right. It gave him nothing of the sort. In future she would be icily formal with him.

When she got back, Erica was further annoyed to find Mrs Roberts in the hall in a state of agitation.

'Mr Macbride told me you'd gone out,' she said, looking at Erica as if she were a wayward child. 'We've been worried about you. Mr Macbride was all worked up.'

'I've only been to the village,' Erica began crossly. 'I'm quite capable of taking care of myself. I actually drove up here from London, you know.'

She was about to add that she often went to the Far East without anybody holding her hand but she thought better of it and, as Alex came in at that moment, she was glad she had held her tongue.

'Oh, if I'd known Dr Thorne was with you, I wouldn't have fretted.' Mrs Roberts sniffed. She had a variety of sniffs, Erica noted. They ranged from disapproval to dismay and this one seemed to be a sniff of deep hurt.

'Don't worry about Erica, Mrs Roberts,' Alex murmured ironically. 'She's from the big city. I can't really think of any time she would need to be rescued. The modern woman is self-sufficient, capable and far-seeing. Erica leaves nothing to chance.'

Erica turned to glare up at him and her wide, annoyed eyes met his dark, complacent stare. He was just too sardonic for words. She turned to storm off and her father came into the hall and looked at them in surprise.

'Why are you all standing here?' he asked, and then his eyes fell on Erica. 'Oh, Erica, you're back. Let's get on. I've had my rest as you ordered so I'm ready to start. Better get changed,' he added, glancing at her. 'You're wet.'

And furious. She cast a reproachful look at Mrs Roberts and went off up the stairs. So much for her father being all worked up! All he wanted to do was get started again but Mrs Roberts had delivered her neatly into Alex's hands by her remarks. Really, she didn't know how he had the nerve to treat her as he did. After all, she was a secretary—as far as he knew. Would he be like this with anyone else who came to work here?

She rather doubted it. Her relationship with Alex had been set from the moment she had first seen him and flown at him in a rage. It had put her at a disadvantage right from the start. She had a very quick, hot shower to drive out the cold and then changed to go back down to the study. Now once again she had given Alex Thorne the right to show his superiority and she hadn't even got the paints.

'I'll get your boots, dear, and dry them out,' Mrs Roberts murmured as they passed in the hall, and Erica went into the study in an almost dazed frame of mind. The housekeeper was behaving as if nothing had happened at all and when Alex came in a few moments later and handed her a hot cup of tea she was just about ready to scream.

Not long ago he had been lecturing her, snarling at her and now he was behaving like a kindly benefactor, none of his important dignity left. She tightened her lips and glared at him, absolutely refusing to say thank you. Not that he was concerned. He was grinning like a Cheshire cat as he went out of the room.

The following day, Erica was in her room when Alex came home. Once again he was early and the first she knew of his arrival was when he knocked at her door and came in as she called out. She had thought it was

Mrs Roberts and her face showed her sudden surge of alarm.

It was a complete flashback to the past. This was her room here, safety—and she had always had to guard her safety carefully. He was a man, big, standing in the doorway, looking at her. Another face superimposed itself over his in her mind and Erica found her heart racing with fear until she forced herself to remember where she was.

'Are you feeling all right?' Alex looked at her closely and didn't seem too satisfied when she assured him that she was fine. Her initial look of fear faded and turned to one of interested fascination when she realised he had his arms full of parcels. There was quite a variety, all balanced on a box, and, seeing her changed looks, Alex astonished her even more by beginning to toss them with enviable accuracy at the bed.

They skimmed across to fall neatly in the middle of the cover and she was too astonished to say anything at all. When he finally came to the box, he put it on the floor and then stood regarding her with amused eyes.

'I went shopping,' he informed her. 'I had a meeting in Newcastle and decided to spare some time to save you from pneumonia.'

'You bought these things for me?' Erica just stood there, not quite knowing what to do. Once again he was behaving in a rather outlandish manner and she didn't know how to react at all. He was not like other people. He made his own rules.

'Mrs Roberts was able to read the size of your boots. For the rest, I made an educated guess—small.'

Erica's face flooded with colour as his words about thermal undies came unwillingly to her mind, and the slow smile that grew on his face told her he was doing a very good imitation of a mind-reader.

'I—I don't know what to say,' she stammered, looking at him with a good deal of embarrassment. 'I don't know you and yet you've...'

'You would only let a lover buy you clothes?' he asked huskily, and Erica was more embarrassed still.

'I—I don't have lovers and—and I didn't mean that at all. It's just that you're—familiar.'

'I accept the rebuke.' He put his hands in his pockets and lounged against the doorframe. He was still in the immaculate suit he had worn when he had left the house this morning and when he looked like that she had to admit that she felt intimidated. 'Maybe I should have changed before I brought the things here,' he said softly when she just stared at him. 'You don't like me to look like this, do you?'

'I have seen men in suits before,' Erica pointed out with an attempt to face him head-on.

'I scare you,' he continued as if she had never spoken. 'When I'm in casual clothes you have no hesitation in taking a verbal swing at me but when I'm like this you're scared.'

Not scared exactly, she corrected him in her mind. He overwhelmed her. He looked spectacularly handsome and somehow his keen, dark eyes took on an even greater intelligence. She was back to feeling outside all this, a prying stranger. Her eyes moved almost secretly to his hands as he moved them from his pockets and stood upright, preparing to leave. Even his hands looked clever, strong, long-fingered and she had a sudden vision of them touching her.

Erica turned away abruptly, refusing to face him as revulsion flooded through her. The memory had come of other hands, big, thick-fingered . . .

'What is it, Erica?' Alex's voice came from right behind her and she knew that her odd behaviour had brought him right into the room now. 'I save people. I don't attack them. You were staring at my hands as if you expected to be strangled.'

'It's not—you.' She was so unnerved by the sudden and unexpected flash of memory that even her voice shook. It had come out of the blue, something she never thought of now. Who was she fooling? She often thought of it in her darkest nightmares.

'Tell me.' He spun her to face him, his voice deeply commanding, but she had never told anyone and she was not about to start now.

'It's nothing,' she managed evenly. 'I felt faint.'

'I'm a doctor, Erica,' he chided softly. 'You didn't feel faint. You felt scared, and if it's not me then who is it?'

'There's nothing to tell,' she said steadily. 'If there was, I wouldn't tell you. I have friends and you're a stranger.'

'A familiar stranger. Don't let that bit escape you.' He turned to the door and looked at her as he got there. 'Open your presents, child,' he suggested quietly. 'They'll drive away the bogeyman.'

'I can't accept presents,' Erica told him desperately. 'I know I need thicker things if I'm to go outside but if you'll tell me how much—'

'Oh, no.' He shook his head and looked at her very much more firmly than she was looking at him. 'You paid for your car repairs and that's all right but these things are a bonus. Under your expert care, my stepfather appears to be thriving. He's taking his rest and he's very happy and free from melancholy. The bonus is for that, and if you keep on about paying I might just change my mind and strangle you after all.'

'I'm only doing my job.'

'And part of mine and part of Mrs Roberts'. The thing is, Erica, you're too damned good at it. I'm afraid you'll not be able to leave when the time is up. I'll invent something for you to do.'

She couldn't stop the smile that came to her lips. Somehow, praise from Alex was like a prize. She looked away, though, and shook her head.

'I only have one month.'

'Why?' His quiet question almost had her telling him about her leave but she stopped herself just in time.

'I have other plans.'

'We'll see.' He gave a low laugh and tapped the box with the toe of one polished shoe. 'These are the boots. They need thick socks. Don't come rushing down complaining that they're too big. There's an art to wearing boots like these. Of course, it helps if you're a northerner but you might just learn. You're probably quite bright when you care to behave normally.'

He went out as quietly as he had come and Erica stared at the closed door. It was astonishing. Nobody had ever treated her in the way that Alex treated her. She looked down at the parcels and felt like a child after all. He seemed to imagine that he had the right to shout at her and chastise her for being out in the cold and then he rewarded her for something she really enjoyed doing. He had left her feeling quite proud of herself.

She almost fell on the parcels and opened them with a certain amount of glee. There were a couple of thick sweaters, one black and one white, two pairs of thick cord trousers and the necessary thick socks. She was greatly relieved to find that he had not ventured into any thermal-undies shopping. He had not forgotten a thick white cap, though. It looked as if it would come down over her eyes.

The last parcel intrigued her and she opened it, expecting some further warm garment to prevent pneumonia. It was a box of watercolours and several brushes and she looked up at the door with an expression of pure happiness on her face. He might be bossy but he didn't forget anything, she thought, and Erica felt pampered. She had never been pampered in her whole life. It made her feel very tearful.

CHAPTER FIVE

THE next morning, Erica was up early, long before she expected her father to put in an appearance. The sun was shining in a clear sky of winter blue, making the snow glitter and dazzle. Even the carpet under her bare feet was warmed by the sunlight that came into the room from the window and she stood there looking at the scene. The harshness had gone from everything and there was only beauty left. All the same it was going to be cold out there, and even though the wind had dropped there would still be that deep chill in the air.

The feelings of last night lingered—the feelings of being pampered, praised and looked upon with a quiet amusement that was almost affectionate. It was the first time Erica had ever felt that. She had always had to watch her step and this had made her sharp, wary. Today she felt unbelievably free and though she knew the feeling would not last she was almost bubbling with it at the moment. She had a tremendous desire to get outside, to make the most of her new, carefree feelings, and she hurried to get dressed.

She pulled out the new clothes and decided that this morning she would begin her working day with a brisk walk in the park. She would take Charlie and try to have that air of calm about her that Alex had. She frowned at herself as she pulled the white sweater over her head. She was in danger of beginning to hero-worship him and it was something she would have to watch. It would be

wise to remember that he suspected her. He had told her
that quite openly.

At first as she got downstairs there was nobody about
and Erica thought that Alex must have already taken the
dog out, but as she looked in the kitchen she saw Charlie
sitting by the stove, his head on his paws in an attitude
of deep patience. He was waiting for his walk and Erica
was delighted to be there first. Alex would not have to
turn out this morning. She would take Charlie for his
run. It was something she could do for Alex.

'That's better!' Mrs Roberts came in and looked at
her with approval. 'Can't be wearing fancy clothes up
here in November. I thought you hadn't brought anything warm to wear.'

It dawned on Erica that Alex had not mentioned his
shopping trip to anyone and she was so grateful that she
beamed at both Mrs Roberts and Charlie.

'Come on, boy,' she coaxed. 'Let's get out into the
snow.' He was on his feet at once and Mrs Roberts gave
her another glance of approval.

'Now, that's a kind action. It will save Dr Thorne from
taking Charlie out. He's got enough to do without
bothering with a dog.'

Erica escaped before the pronouncement turned into
a serious discussion of ill health and Alex's saintly importance. She opened the back door and Charlie raced
out, bounding round her legs and making short, sharp
forays into the hedges, coming back with his black nose
covered in snow. Normally, he paid little attention to her
but today she could have been the most important person
in his life.

The chill in the air brought colour to her cheeks and
Erica almost felt that she could bound along beside the
dog. It was an entirely new feeling, a feeling of safety,

and she crunched through the crisp snow with a smile on her lips. Being so well wrapped up was unusual for her and after a few minutes the thick woollen cap was just too much; she pulled it off, letting her red hair swing free down over her shoulders.

Charlie suddenly barked and began to race back the way they had come and when Erica looked round to find out why she saw Alex making his way towards them, his tall figure outlined against the bright sky and snow. She shielded her eyes from the sun and watched him. It was funny that her first instinct was to avoid him. He made her feel unsure of herself because his attitude often robbed her of the ability to fight and it was never easy to behave naturally with him when she was constantly aware of her deceit in this house.

As the days had gone by and she'd found that she was liking her father more and more, Erica's conscience had had a hard struggle to be silent. Alex, too, was treating her as if she had been here for a long time but she was always certain that his anger would be very real if he discovered her genuine reason for being here. She dreaded the embarrassment of it because now she would not be able to defend herself by a sharp attack of temper. She didn't blame her father any more and raging her way out of it would be impossible.

At the moment, however, it was hopeless to try to avoid Alex. He had seen her before she'd seen him. If she shot off hastily he was just going to think her more odd than ever.

'You,' Alex said sternly as he drew close, 'are usurping my position. I am chief dog-handler.' He was smiling at her and Erica couldn't help smiling back.

'I thought I was doing you a favour,' she told him pertly. 'Mrs Roberts thinks you're too important and hard-pressed to spare time with a dog.'

He grimaced wryly.

'Please don't tell me she tricked you into coming out here with one of her dire tales of hospital stress.'

'Well, she started,' Erica confessed, 'but actually I was already on my way to the back door with Charlie and I escaped.'

'So you really were doing me a favour?'

'No.' Erica squinted up at him in the bright sunlight. 'It was an excuse to get out into the fresh air.'

'Which is why I walk him,' Alex said drily. 'Poor Charlie, you're just an excuse.'

The dog jumped up, landing snow-covered paws all over him, and Alex began to throw snowballs for Charlie to chase. It looked like fun and before long Erica was joining in—the first time she had done anything foolishly spontaneous for years. They were both racing after the dog, aiming the snowballs ahead of him, and a few breathless minutes later Erica tripped over the hidden root of a tree and fell flat, landing on her back with her hair in the cold snow.

She was still laughing but when she looked up Alex was standing over her, a giant with dark, amused eyes that roamed over her face slowly. The merriment died in Erica and she wondered what she was doing here behaving like an idiot when she should have been very cautious with this man. He already suspected her. One false move and she would be at his mercy.

'Better get up. A good deal of the body's warmth is lost through the head.' He held out his hand to her. 'Isn't this the third time I've rescued you? If I didn't know better, I would think you were doing it deliberately.'

'What do you mean?' Erica ignored his outstretched hand and looked up at him crossly. 'You know perfectly well that each time it's been an accident.'

'Some people really enjoy being rescued,' he murmured ironically. 'Some people even plan it.'

'Really?' Erica was incensed by his soft sarcasm. It was making her feel more foolish than ever. She reached for his helping hand and when his fingers closed round hers she gave a very hard tug. He had not been expecting it and the footing in the snow was not too firm. She succeeded in overbalancing him and it was only as she saw him falling that Erica realised he was about to fall on her.

She gave a small, panicky cry and tried to move but her reaction was not nearly fast enough; Alex landed half over her, his own reactions saving her from the worst of his weight. Even so, most of the breath was knocked from her and Erica looked up helplessly into the face that was now so close to her own.

'Very amusing, Miss Linton,' he congratulated her softly. '*Now* what do you plan to do?' The dark eyes held hers unswervingly and Erica's heart began to pound like a hammer. A great surge of reaction hit her. It was a wild mixture of fear, embarrassment and excitement.

She was unable to sort out one feeling from another. She was aware of the weight and strength of the body almost over hers, the silence of the snow-covered landscape, and the incongruity of her position was forgotten as she felt the old fear winning. Her muscles tightened, her dark blue eyes widened and the original look of triumph faded from her face. Her arms were trapped and she could feel a frenzy of panic growing.

'No! Let me get up!'

There was every sign of her growing fear on her face and Alex's eyes narrowed with concerned interest as he looked down at her.

'I'm only here because you pulled me here,' he reminded her quietly. 'This was your idea, Erica.'

'I've got to get up! Move! Move!' She tensed up with fear and his hand came to her face, warm against her cold cheek.

'Shh,' he said softly. 'I have every intention of getting up.' He moved, rolling away and standing in one movement, and this time she didn't get the chance to accept his hand; he reached down and almost lifted her bodily.

Erica was shaking, too filled with shock to feel any shame at her bizarre reaction. For the moment, she felt unable to take even one step and, worse still, her eyes began to fill with tears. It was a long time since she had felt like this, a long time since she had allowed any panic to grip her. She had taken good care never to get herself into any situation where her old fear could surface. It had been her odd relationship with Alex and her feelings of freedom and gratitude on this sunny morning that had lulled her into doing so.

He tilted her face with one warm hand.

'Is it just me or does everyone get the same reaction?' he asked quietly.

'It—it's a sort of phobia, I expect,' she managed in an uneven voice. She bit hard at her lip to stop the trembling and one tear drifted to her cheek as she blinked her eyes.

'Claustrophobia or a phobia of men?' he persisted, and one hard red face came into her mind, hard, lascivious eyes, hard hands with thick fingers.

'Not—not all men.'

'So it's me?' he asked wryly, and she looked at him with wild eyes, still wet with tears.

'*No!* It was just... it was just... I was trapped! I couldn't get away!' He was looking at her with pity, like a doctor, and she snatched her face from his grasp, turning her head, colour coming back to her pale cheeks.

'Don't look at me like that,' she ordered shakily. 'I'm not a hysterical freak and I don't need your medical assistance.' She turned back to face him, taking a slow, calming breath. 'I brought it on myself and I'm sorry. I'm sorry, too, if I embarrassed you. It—it had nothing to do with you at all. I don't feel scared of you and—'

'Let's see.' He reached out for her, gathering her close before she had any inkling of his intention. She found herself wrapped in his arms and her hands came instantly to his chest, fight her first thought.

Alex just looked down at her intently, his dark eyes assessing, and Erica felt her hands relaxing, the instantaneous panic fading.

'Very good,' he praised quietly, but he didn't offer to release her. Her fast breathing slowed and she was able to look back at him steadily.

'You see?' she pointed out. 'It had nothing to do with you.'

'Prove it,' he insisted softly, and before she could move his head bent to hers and his lips brushed her startled mouth and then captured it firmly.

Erica's small, shocked cry was muffled against his lips. This was something she had never even thought of. It was true that her fascination with Alex had grown during the time she had been here and it was true also that she had recently chided herself when she had found the inclination growing to turn him into some sort of hero, but she had never imagined any other feelings.

The pressure of his kiss increased and when she made no effort to resist his arms gathered her closer. This time, the familiar feelings of fear and disgust didn't materialise and Erica was so stunned by the new emotions flooding through her that she remained pliant and soft in his arms.

He lifted his head slightly, looking down at her with dark, probing eyes.

'More proof needed, Erica,' he murmured, and when his lips closed over hers again she found herself moving closer, searching for some elusive feeling of contentment that was hovering just at the back of her mind. She had never been close to anyone ever. She had always made quite certain that nobody could be close to her because she had always known what would happen. The panic would grow and she would fight.

Now there was no fight in her and when his mouth searched hers warmly she felt an overwhelming urge to kiss him back. Her hands crept higher, making their way to his neck by some strange decision of their own, and when her fingers lightly touched his face Alex lifted his head and smiled down at her.

'So, the tigress is a lamb after all. Now tell me about the panic,' he ordered quietly.

The order, so softly spoken, brought her back into her own character swiftly and colour flooded her face. She was no longer puzzled by his actions. He had been conducting an experiment, observing her, *curing* her!

She pulled free and glared at him, forcing her trembling legs to hold her stiffly upright.

'I never agreed to take part in any clinical trials, Dr Thorne,' she snapped. 'You can cross me off your list and look for another patient!'

Erica spun away but he reached out and captured her again, laughing into her angry face.

'Don't be a little idiot.' He brushed the snow away that still clung to her hair. 'Put your cap on and behave yourself.'

She shrugged herself free, outrage written across her face. He was standing there, towering over her, grinning at her, and the dog was sitting in the snow watching. As far as she could tell, the dog was grinning at her too. It certainly looked like it.

'Leave me alone!' she shouted at Alex. 'You too!' She aimed a violent look at Charlie and stormed off towards the house. She could hear Alex laughing and she walked on, leaving him standing there. He could come back by himself. She hadn't asked him to walk with her in the first place.

It soon became apparent, however, that he was not coming back. He didn't catch up with her and when she risked an angry glance behind her after a while Alex had walked almost out of sight, the dog running round him in hysterical circles of delight. Being so important must be dangerous, she thought furiously. He was so accustomed to people fawning over him, hanging onto his every word that he felt he could practise his medical skills on anyone to hand.

Erica stamped back to the house and went up to her room to change. She threw the thick garments onto the floor and had a hot shower all over again. She had not even stopped to have breakfast before she had taken the dog out. It was not an experiment she would repeat. She took great care in dressing, putting on a soft woollen dress that was an exact match for her eyes and brushing her hair into a shining curtain of deep red.

She frowned at herself and looked with suspicion at
the glow on her face. It was the healthy walk, of course,
but she was not about to let any high-ranking doctor
imagine that he had induced it. She stood and grimly
worked her hair into a long, shining plait. It hung down
her back and left her face looking much more severe. It
would do very nicely, and she went down for her
breakfast with a severe expression to match.

Alex was already eating and he stood politely and then
handed her the toast without any comment at all. A sur-
reptitious glance assured her that he was not laughing;
in fact, he looked about as severe as she did and Erica
felt a stab of anxiety. Had she behaved normally? What
would an ordinary secretary have done under the
circumstances?

Mrs Roberts came in with the food and the meal was
conducted in silence. It was very unnerving but Erica
became more and more annoyed as the silence continued. She knew he was doing it deliberately but all the
same it was getting under her guard. When he murmured politely and got up, leaving the room in the same
silent manner, she was left in a turmoil of rage and
embarrassment.

Somehow or other, it all seemed to be her fault, and
even if she was the only one thinking it she still couldn't
shake off the guilt. If she hadn't foolishly pulled him
down into the snow, if she hadn't struggled and
panicked...

It was only as Mrs Roberts came in later to collect the
plates that Erica really felt small and insignificant.

'Poor Dr Thorne,' Mrs Roberts mourned. 'Did you
hear the phone call just a minute or two before breakfast?
One of those poor souls died in the night.'

Erica jumped up and walked out, remorse almost choking her. That was why he had been so silent. But how could she have known? He just didn't behave like other people. He seemed to live by some peculiar set of rules that she didn't understand.

He was almost at the front door, dressed ready for the hospital, and Erica quickly went after him.

'I'm sorry,' she called out impulsively. 'I didn't know...'

'About what?' He turned to glance at her and there was no sign of his usual amused look.

'Mrs Roberts said—'

'Don't take the cares of the world on your shoulders, Erica,' he advised her grimly. 'Leave it to Mrs Roberts. She was born with the necessary state of mind.' He walked out, shutting the door, and she was still standing there when his car pulled away from the front of the house. The strange and exciting intimacy they had shared earlier might well have never happened. Now he was another person, someone she didn't know at all, and from the look on his face he didn't know her either.

Just before lunch, Erica saw another car arrive. It was a rather flashy and expensive sports car and a very small blonde got out, smiling up at the house as if she was very glad to be there. She was really lovely, Erica mused, watching her as she came to the house.

She was fashionably dressed but much more expensively than Erica could manage. A fur coat was flung round her shoulders and it was real. The blonde hair was short, expertly cut, and the suit she was wearing was obviously worth more than Erica could ever afford.

She came up the steps and after that Erica couldn't see her but moments later she burst into the study, coming across to Erica's father and throwing her arms round his neck before he could recover from his surprise.

'Uncle Philip! I'm here!' she exclaimed, and Erica was astonished at the sharp burst of annoyance she felt at this stranger acting so affectionately with her father. She had to stifle it. After all, *she* was the stranger here—the deceitful stranger—and she had no right to allow any feelings at all to colour her attitude to anyone who knew her father better than she did. Alex's familiarity with her father did not annoy her. It seemed natural and right. This girl called him Uncle Philip and, after all, what did she know about his life except the things her mother had told her? She got on with her work and tried not to look.

'Fiona! We never expected to see you in this weather,' Philip said as he extricated himself from the great hug he was getting. 'How long is the visit going to be this time?'

'Oh, Uncle Philip, you're chastising me. You know I can't stay up in the wilds for long even in summer. I had to come, though. I miss Alex so much and this week he hasn't rung me once.'

There was a spoiled, pouting air about her and Erica glanced up and saw a matching expression on her face.

'It's been a busy week for Alex,' Philip said soberly. 'He's had two very difficult cases. We've hardly seen him ourselves. Isn't that right, Erica?'

He was politely bringing her into the conversation and the bright blue eyes of Fiona turned on Erica for the first time. Until now she had studiously ignored the fact that there was another person in the room but now she didn't have any choice. She stared at Erica coolly, her eyes making a quick inventory of Erica's appearance.

Erica felt as if her own clothes had been price-tagged and dismissed at once. The gaze then turned to her red hair and Erica wished heartily that she had not child-ishly put her hair into a severe plait, because that was dismissed too.

'A secretary, Uncle Philip? You've acquired status. Is she from the village?'

'Erica is from London,' Philip Macbride said, a note of annoyance entering his voice at this attitude. 'She lives here at the moment. I hope she'll be living here for a long time, too, because she's helping me and doing me a lot of good into the bargain. Alex thinks she's won-derful for me.'

The pale blue eyes narrowed at the mention of Alex and Erica was once again given a swift glance of in-spection before Fiona straightened up and made for the door.

'Must see Mrs Roberts,' she announced. 'I hope I can have that gorgeous room this time.'

'You never stay long enough,' Philip pointed out. 'Alex won't have Mrs Roberts put to extra work for a quick visit. In any case, Erica has that room.'

From the look on Fiona's face this was the very last straw and she grimaced in the same spoiled manner before she drifted out on a cloud of expensive perfume.

'Alex's cousin, Fiona Croft,' Philip murmured as the door closed. 'She's an actress and she doesn't really have the time to drive up here but she can't stay away from Alex for too long. She's full of hope in that direction.'

'His cousin?' Erica asked, and she couldn't quite keep the surprise from her voice.

'Not exactly,' Philip corrected her. 'I suppose she's a relative many times removed but when it suits her she's his cousin; that's if she's not getting it all her own way. I understand that in London she's his fiancée—the fiancée of an important consultant, you see. It gives her more status. Though, unless I'm mistaken, she wouldn't mind it at all if it were true. She certainly works at it. I often think Alex will give in from sheer exhaustion, although he really is fond of her.'

Erica found that this was something she didn't want to know and she got on with her typing more vigorously. She had been beginning to feel almost at home here, only Alex's calm air of authority when she was dressed for work causing her any anxiety. Now she felt outside it all again, rather lost. She had nothing to do with these people. They lived in a world she could never hope to reach.

The brief flash of pleasure she had felt when her father had mentioned Alex's praise about her effect on him now simply vanished. Fiona was part of their world, while she could not even acknowledge her own father.

When her duties were over, Erica disappeared to her room and stayed there, even worried about coming down for dinner. She had to surface, though. If she did not, her father would want to know why and if Alex was home for the meal then he would show no hesitation in coming to get her. He had enough problems. But then, the sight of Fiona would no doubt cheer him up.

Erica looked through her wardrobe and decided that she could not compete at all with the fashionable glitter of Fiona Croft. She put on a pair of tight trousers with a long matching top and after looking at herself carefully she didn't even bother to brush out the plait. She went out of her room as she was and walked rather gloomily to the stairs.

Before she got there Alex came up them, and after one quick glance at her he stopped and looked at her unwaveringly.

'Is it part of the plan or sheer accident?' he asked rather irascibly, and Erica was completely taken by surprise.

'I don't—' she began, but he cut in ruthlessly.

'Know what I mean? I think you do, Miss Linton. If that hairstyle is supposed to make you look like an untouchable little waif then, as far as I'm concerned, it's succeeding. You may like to know that I didn't intend to touch you in any case. Brushing your hair out will be perfectly safe.'

Erica just stared at him, quite stunned by his unexpected and unfair attack. He was always fair, and why he was taking this attitude now she didn't know. It was annoying in any case and she glared at him.

'My hairstyle is my affair,' she snapped, 'but if you really are so interested then I'd better tell you that it's supposed to be severe.'

'I see,' he growled. 'I'm not being warned off, I'm being frightened off.'

'It has nothing to do with you,' Erica insisted, agitated by rising annoyance, 'but if your conscience is troubling you about this morning then don't let it bother you. I quite understand that it was all part of your medical research.'

His lips quirked in amusement, the anger dying out of his face.

'Perhaps,' he murmured, his dark eyes skimming her face. 'As to my conscience, it never troubles me.'

'It does,' Erica said thoughtlessly. 'You were upset about the news from the hospital this morning.'

The smile died out of his eyes and he took hold of her arm with the usual strong grip, jerking her towards him.

'You think I should just shrug it off?' he asked coldly. 'When I've fought for a life I like to win. Should I behave like a machine?'

'No,' she whispered. She shook her head, the anger simply draining away as sympathy came into her eyes. 'I know you couldn't be like that and—and if I were ill I would want somebody like you to care about me.'

His eyes narrowed on her, intent and searching.

'Doesn't anyone care about you, Erica?' he asked softly, and she looked away, her cheeks beginning to flush.

'I was just making a point. I was...' She looked back at him in frustration. 'You make me say all sorts of things I don't mean,' she complained. 'You get me confused.'

'How am I to catch you otherwise?' He suddenly grinned at her, and just as she expected him to let go of her arm he bent his head and kissed her. It was a quick, teasing gesture but her face flushed more deeply still and she stood bemused as he let her go.

'You shouldn't do things like that. You don't know me.' Her voice trembled slightly and his grin turned into a mocking smile.

'Of course I do, Erica. You're my prize patient. You occupy my thoughts almost all the time.'

'Darling! What are you up to?' Fiona's voice cut in abruptly and they both turned to see her standing at the top of the stairs. It was obvious from her sharp tone that she had been there long enough to see the quick, teasing kiss but Alex looked at her calmly.

'I'm dealing with Erica,' he assured her. 'Erica can be quite difficult. She needs a lot of attention.'

'You were supposed to be getting changed for dinner,' Fiona complained in that pouting voice, and he nodded in amusement.

'I was about to but Erica sidetracked me. She needed me. However, I'll get changed now.'

'Can I wait with you, darling?' Fiona pleaded, and he shot her a glance of keen amusement.

'Certainly. You can sit cross-legged outside my door. That's where the dutiful wait.'

'You always tease me cruelly,' she muttered.

And Alex glanced at Erica's embarrassed face and asked, 'Do I tease you cruelly too, Erica? I really must be careful or I'll never sort you out.'

Fiona advanced with very grim determination. She had no intention of being left out and Alex looked with narrowed eyes at Erica's open distress.

'Run along, little waif,' he said softly. 'You can wait at the door too if you like but I think you would be out of your league.'

Erica fled. She was out of her league here and she knew it very well. The thought of dinner with Fiona sitting there glaring at her was unnerving but she straightened her back and walked down the stairs with a little more dignity than she felt.

This was ridiculous. This was nothing at all to do with the reason for her stay here. She had come to find her father, to get to know him. She was not here to be drawn into the peculiar whirlpool of emotion that Alex was creating.

The trouble was that he had to be faced daily. There was no escape from him unless she simply abandoned her father and his work. She knew that if she did that her father would be upset and by now she cared too much even to think of hurting him. She would have to learn to deal with Alex. Now there was Fiona too. Erica suspected that Fiona would not leave quite so readily this time. The other woman didn't like any sort of competition as far as Alex was concerned.

It would have been amusing if she had been able to watch from the side and not be involved. Competition! Fiona must be really keen on capturing Alex if she could even begin to think that there was any sort of competition in this house at the moment. Fiona glittered like the Snow Queen while *she* was nothing more than a waif! Alex's taunting words came back and she clenched her hands in annoyance. Why didn't he just leave her alone and get on with his job? Heavens, he had enough to do without taking on any more commitments.

Of course, he suspected her. That was something he would not ignore. He would not let the subject drop no matter how long she stayed here, and the longer she stayed, the greater the danger. One day he would find out. His intelligence was alarming and he would search and pry until he was satisfied. That was why he treated her in such a familiar manner. He knew she was in a perpetually dazed state after any encounter with him. One day she would forget to watch her step. He was banking on it, confusing her with quiet deliberation. One day he would win, and she would have to leave very fast when that day came.

CHAPTER SIX

FIONA stayed on but it was very apparent that she was bored and irritated by the calm, quiet atmosphere of the household. In many ways it was a revelation to Erica. She had always felt that she did not fit in here and when Fiona had arrived Erica had sadly mourned the fact that the newcomer was more used to her father than she was herself. Fiona also had that certain air of polish that made her seem right for Alex.

Now, though, after several displays of petulance and many utterances about the slowness of life up here in the frozen north, Fiona was showing herself to be utterly out of place, too, but for very different reasons.

Erica loved the quiet old house and the tranquillity of a set routine. She had become accustomed to watching Alex leave in the morning and to waiting for him to come in at night. She always knew if he had had a bad day by the look on his face, even when he hid his problems. It was becoming a joy to work with her father and surreptitiously to keep an eye on his health.

Erica didn't fit in because of her deception. She was treated like a member of the household by everyone but inside she was constantly edgy and on her guard against discovery. She also felt a long way from Alex's world of wealth and importance and knew that when she left here, even if she escaped detection, she would be nothing more than a faint quirk to Alex's lips if he remembered her at all. She would have her father's gratitude but that was all she could expect.

Fiona, on the other hand, expected everything. She demanded constant attention and pouted when it was not forthcoming. If Alex returned tired and quiet she didn't even have the sense to keep out of his way.

'If you worked in London I could see you every day,' she complained on her last evening at Keresford House.

'That would also be true if you worked up here,' Alex pointed out wryly. They were having dinner and Fiona held the centre-stage position as she had done every evening. Now she looked at Alex in frustration, her pouting very close to actual temper.

'You know I can't work up here!' she exclaimed. 'How could I ever hope to get parts in this place? It's further than the back of beyond.'

Erica had thought that when she'd first come but now the tranquillity had become almost part of her life.

'That's true,' Alex agreed drily. 'Any further north and you would drop off the end of the world.'

'I'm really serious,' Fiona snapped. 'Seeing each other like this is ridiculous. We could be together in London and it would do your career a lot of good.'

'I do good where it's needed,' Alex said with a sudden cold note to his voice. 'The sick are not clustered in London. In any case, my life is here, my home is here.'

'It's where your heart is that matters,' Fiona reminded him with a long look of cloying affection. She was changing her tack at Alex's suddenly cold rebuff and his dark brows raised sardonically.

'I don't have a heart, do I, Erica?' His eyes were mockingly amused again as he met Erica's embarrassed gaze. 'I simply pry into minds.'

Erica was saved from further embarrassment when the telephone in the hall rang, and Alex was on his feet at once as he went to answer it. Her father took the chance to leave also.

'No coffee for me, Erica,' he muttered. 'Tell Mrs Roberts, will you? I—er—have something to do.'

Erica knew exactly what he had to do. He had to escape. Since Fiona Croft had been here the peace had been shattered, and although she found it difficult herself the effect it was having on her father was much more traumatic. He was often agitated when Fiona began her lengthy speeches and this evening she had come to the very edge of argument. It was quite obvious that this state of affairs upset him.

'Are you all right?' Erica asked gently, and he patted her hand as he stood to leave.

'Fine. Don't worry. I'll probably see you later.'

When he had gone there was no one else at all to take the brunt of Fiona's tongue and when Erica looked up the bright blue eyes were watching her coldly.

'You seem to have made quite a comfortable little place for yourself here, Miss Linton,' she remarked. 'Uncle Philip seems to rely on you entirely.'

'He simply needs my typing skills,' Erica assured her quickly.

'According to Alex, you're invaluable. Of course, he only means until Uncle Philip has finished his funny old book. I expect you'll be back off to where you came from then.'

'Most likely,' Erica assured her quietly. Most certainly, she added to herself. There would be no further excuse for being here.

'What a pity that you'll miss the summer here. It can be quite spectacular and the sea is so wild and free in these parts. When Alex and I are married he'll come to

London of course, in spite of what he says, but we'll always keep this house.'

Erica knew it would probably come true. Her father had said that Fiona worked at it relentlessly and she had seen that for herself. He had also said that Alex was very fond of her. He must be. She was always throwing her arms round him and even when he was tired he never tried to stop her. Erica was saved from any reply because Alex came back in at that moment and he did not look amused any more.

'The call is for you,' he told Erica. 'Apparently your boyfriend is concerned about you. His flight has just landed.'

Erica's face flushed with anxiety. Why, oh, why hadn't she been in touch with Jeremy before this? She had intended to ring him as soon as she discovered the danger here. There was no knowing what he had said to Alex. She hurried out to the phone, carefully shutting the door behind her, and Alex's dark eyes followed her all the way.

'Oh, Jeremy! I thought I told you not to contact me here? I asked you not to before I even left London.' Erica started straight away before he could even say hello. 'I've been going to ring you to remind you about it but I just haven't had the time.'

'What's wrong with you?' Jeremy asked huffily. 'You're not in prison up there. I don't know what you're doing, Erica, but it comes to something when I can't even phone.'

'Look, I'm sorry,' Erica soothed. 'When I get back to London I'll tell you all about it but for now I really must keep my head down.'

'Well, it's up to you,' Jeremy muttered, a little placated by her tone. 'As it happens, I'm doing you a favour. I knew it was pretty hush-hush up there and I wouldn't have rung at all. I think you'll be glad that I did, though, when you've heard my news.'

'What news?' Erica stood by the phone, gradually letting her pulses slow to normal. After all, she had every right to receive phone calls and if Alex thought that Jeremy was her boyfriend it didn't much matter. As to his plane having landed, for all Alex knew he might have just been abroad, unless, of course, Jeremy had announced that he was the flight engineer on the aircraft that Erica normally flew on.

She suddenly came out of her anxious musings as she heard her mother mentioned.

'What?' Her agitation returned at once and Jeremy patiently had to repeat his words.

'I said that I'd bumped into your mother by sheer chance. I asked how you were and she told me she hadn't seen you. I'm afraid I let it slip that you were on some secret mission to Northumberland and had taken unpaid leave. She was very interested. She wants to see you, urgently.'

'Why?' Erica asked suspiciously, and she almost heard his shrug of resignation.

'How should I know? All I can tell you is that she really pricked up her ears. Seeing you at once sounded more like an order than a request. She demanded your telephone number.'

'You didn't give her it!'

'Said I'd mislaid it. Spur-of-the-moment thinking. I did say, however, that I would find it and call you. She insisted on setting a date for meeting you. Monday.'

'But it's Friday now so that only gives me two days!' Erica exclaimed, and he sighed at her over the phone.

'Is that my fault? I only saw her this morning. Honestly, Erica, I think you'd better come. She looked as if she might just come up there and explore Northumberland looking for you.'

Erica believed him. When her mother set her mind on something, she persisted doggedly. And there was not much doubt about why she wanted a meeting. She would have fathomed out why it was necessary for Erica to be up here.

There was no knowing what she would do if the meeting didn't take place. After all, *she* had found her father and there was no reason to suppose that her mother could not do exactly the same thing. She was an intelligent woman and very, very stubborn.

When Erica fully replaced the receiver, she stood thinking, her mind given entirely to this latest problem. Would her mother be able to track her down to Keresford House? It was more than likely. Before she had re-married, her mother had been a secretary with one of the television companies. She might very well have contacts there still.

If she came up here it would be horrendous. Her mother was quite hard and never much given to holding her tongue. She might even demand to see her ex-husband and spend some time goading him about his long-lost daughter. Erica winced, even though it had not come to pass. Her imagination was running riot but she couldn't help it.

She would just have to think of some excuse and go to meet her mother on Monday. She would have to think of something before the weekend was over and the only thing she could think of at all was that she wanted to see Jeremy. It sounded feasible that she should be pining for her boyfriend. She would work it all out and then tell her father. More deceit. She bit her lip and felt very unhappy.

'Erica?'

When she looked up with a guilty start she found Alex standing watching her. He was by the door of the little room where they watched television and she hadn't heard him go in there. What had he overheard of her conversation? And where was Fiona?

She just stared at him and he looked back unwaveringly.

'What's wrong?' he asked quietly. 'Don't bother to say, Nothing. I know your expressions. Something is troubling you.'

'It—it's just that I never expected a phone call,' she said with a good deal of hesitation. 'I—I didn't know that Jeremy would be back.'

'So?' He just went on staring at her, the concern dying from his eyes.

'I have to go to London on Monday,' she said hurriedly, deciding to get it over with now. 'He—er—he's only got the one day and then he's leaving again.'

'Quite a problem,' he murmured coldly. 'I imagine Philip will give you the day off. He seems to dote on you. That should take care of everything.'

'Do you mind?' She looked at him worriedly and he raised dark brows in sardonic surprise.

'Me? Why should I? You're not working for me. Basically it has nothing to do with me at all.'

Alex turned and went back into the room and Erica could hear Fiona's voice before the door closed. They were cosily settled in there as they had been every evening and she went to look in on her father before she escaped to her own room and privacy.

He was in his study but he was not working. He was just looking at the drawings and obviously hiding there to shut out the rest of the household.

'Please don't work,' Erica begged, her eyes anxiously scanning his face. He didn't look too good and she felt a great surge of rage at the thought of Fiona Croft's coming here and upsetting her father. Her very presence disturbed the place even if she said nothing at all, and Fiona was never silent.

'I'm not working, Erica,' he assured her tiredly. 'I'm just keeping out of the way. I find Fiona exhausting. I was just looking at my illustrations.'

It reminded Erica about her efforts of the past few days. She had been tinting the discarded sketches in her time off and in the evenings when Alex and Fiona were in the cosy little sitting room. Her father had no idea about the sketches and she thought it might just cheer him up.

'Stay here,' she ordered mysteriously. 'I have something to show you.'

'You're very good for me, Erica,' he told her, his face lighting up. 'I have this strange feeling that I've known you before.'

Erica smiled and escaped. It must be some deep instinct, almost like the homing instinct of animals, because she also felt that she had always known her father. She ran up to her room and seconds later she was tearing back down the stairs with the finished pictures in her hand.

Alex and Fiona were just coming out of the sitting room and she didn't even bother to look at them. She went quickly to her father's study and closed the door behind her. In this room, *they* were the intruders. It belonged to her father and she worked with him. She didn't see the look in Alex's eyes as he watched her disappear.

'I've been doing these,' Erica told her father breathlessly. She put them in front of him on his desk and stood at his side, bending over to watch. She was terribly nervous about it, wondering if he would be annoyed that she had meddled with his work, even though he had said she could have them.

He spread them out over the desktop and regarded them silently, and when she bent further over and risked a small peep at his face Erica was delighted to see that he was completely engrossed.

'They're fantastic,' he murmured to himself. 'I can see now why I thought they were wrong. Your shading has given a good deal of depth to them, a roundness to the animals that I'd missed out.'

'You haven't missed it out in the ones you're having printed,' Erica insisted firmly. 'It was only these few.'

'All the same,' he muttered. He glanced up at her as she hovered over him, almost hugging herself with glee. 'I know it's asking a lot but do you feel like doing this to all the sketches, Erica?'

'Oh! I might spoil them. They're good enough to go as they are. It would be too risky.'

'It's not much of a risk by the look of these. They'll be a lot better if you tint them like this,' he insisted. 'I know you've been doing it in your spare time but...'

'I've loved every minute of it,' Erica assured him. 'It's given me something to do in the evenings, especially since...'

She stopped guiltily but her father followed her train of thought with no difficulty.

'I know,' he murmured, giving her the same sort of wry look that Alex handed out. 'I've been hard-pressed to stay put and be civilised. Maybe I've been out in Africa far too long.'

'And maybe you're too ill to face a battering,' Erica put in firmly, disregarding good manners when she thought of his having wearily to face that barrage every day.

'Will you tint the others?' he persisted, and she gave him a gleeful smile.

'Yes,' she said.

The door opened at that moment as Alex came in and Erica and her father looked up at him. They were both still in the same position and Erica was still leaning over. They must have had an almost identical look of delight on their faces because Alex stopped suddenly, his eyes going from one to the other. There was a growing enlightenment on his face that worried Erica at once.

'Alex. Just look at these!' Philip said excitedly. 'Right out of the blue this wonderful girl has produced them and boosted my flagging spirits. I've asked her to do the lot. My goodness, they're so good that they'll sell the book by themselves.'

Alex came forward slowly and his narrow-eyed look of consideration moved from Erica to the sketches. She watched him with as much anxiety as she had watched her father and she saw his lips finally tilt in reluctant admiration.

'Talented,' he murmured. 'So this is why you wanted the paints. They're very good indeed. Professional.'

'Mr Macbride did the sketches,' Erica said hastily. 'I just coloured them in. A child could have done it.'

'Don't sell yourself short, Erica,' her father interrupted. 'No child could have done them. These are very skilfully executed. They really are professional, as Alex says.'

Erica carefully filed them away. She had also intended to ask about Monday but it looked as if Alex was going to stay so she wanted to go quickly. When she did go, she found him beside her, opening the door for her and stepping out of the study when she did.

There was no escaping him and as he closed the door behind them he grasped her arm, forcing her to stay there. Erica looked up at him and her spirits sank when she saw his eyes narrow and look back with a vengeance.

'How much did you know about my stepfather before you came here?' he asked coldly, his eyes pinning her fast.

'I had his letter. I told you that. I must have read about his life in Africa somewhere but apart from that—'

'You're lying, Erica,' he said with menacing quiet. 'There's something going off here that I still can't work out, but one thing I do know—you're lying.'

'Why should I lie?' Erica challenged, unable to escape and unwilling to face another inquisition. 'I'd like to know what I've gained out of it, apart from hard work.'

'You've moved in under his heart,' Alex grated. 'If you left he would be too depressed to do anything. You're a good deal more than his Girl Friday. He cares about you. He even whispers to you about Fiona when he thinks I'm not looking.'

'Are you surprised?' Erica countered sharply. 'I would imagine that it's either whisper or explode.'

'You don't approve of Fiona?' he asked with a change to silky interrogation, and Erica glowered up at him.

'She has nothing to do with me!'

'And everything to do with me?' he enquired in the same smooth tone.

'She's your fiancée!'

'Not yet,' Alex corrected her softly. 'You can speak your mind with no worry about reprisals as things are as yet unofficial.'

'All right,' Erica snapped. 'You must be able to see for yourself that she's worn your stepfather out. He's not nearly as well as he was. You tell me to watch him, order me to get him to rest and then you...'

'Bring that hussy into the house?' he enquired suavely. 'Do we have melodrama here, my little cat?'

'I am not your little cat,' Erica pointed out hotly, her cheeks flushing with annoyance. 'I'm speaking out because you invited me to do so. If the interrogation is over, would you kindly return my arm and I'll be on my way?'

'I let you go with some reluctance,' he admitted as his hold on her arm slackened. 'Never mind. Fiona leaves tomorrow morning and then we'll be back to our normal routine. I'll be able to give you some close attention.'

'I don't want any attention,' Erica told him with very visible frustration. 'I just want to get on with my job.'

'And which job is that, Erica?' he asked softly. 'The one you're doing openly or the one you're doing in secret?'

He had managed it again. She was almost shaking with nervous anger and she turned her head, once again afraid to look at him.

'Please leave me alone,' she said in little more than a whisper. 'I just can't go on here if you don't.'

'I can't promise to leave you alone,' he said quietly. 'I seem to be incapable of leaving you alone.' He spun her to face him and she could see an equal amount of frustration on his face. 'Maybe Philip is not the only one you've got to or maybe you intrigue me too much to be ignored.'

He swept her towards him and this time the kiss he gave her was neither teasing nor healing. It was an almost savage kiss of exasperation. His lips moved over hers with no apology, in fact there was almost hostility, and when he let her go she was trembling and burning with the same excitement that had grown when he had kissed her in the snow.

'And don't bother to point out in your irritating little way that I'm a doctor and should behave accordingly,' he rasped, staring down at her angrily. 'I damned well know that myself!'

Erica pulled free and ran up the stairs without looking back, but she knew he wasn't watching her. She heard the door of the sitting room bang shut and she wondered angrily if he was about to tell Fiona that he had been kissing the hired help.

He would not have had the opportunity because, as Erica rounded the top of the stairs, Fiona was blocking her way. She was in her dressing gown—a frothy creation of lace and silk—and she confronted Erica angrily.

'He may like to kiss you to amuse himself,' she hissed, 'but he's mine. He always has been. Leave him alone!'

'Chance would be a fine thing!' Erica snapped, and she pushed past the other woman and went to her room. She did a bit of door-banging herself and then she almost fell on the bed, her legs shaking as if she had run for miles.

Being tempted to look upon him as a hero was one thing. Being bemused when he had kissed her in the snow and later on in the passage was another. But to actually like it and feel like staying there for more when he had kissed her like a savage and left her with bruised lips was another thing entirely.

The excitement was still racing through her and she buried her head in the pillow and gave a soft moan. Now what did she do? If she left, her father would be bitterly disappointed and she had only just now made him another promise. If she stayed she would soon become addicted to Alex.

In any case, he would find her out. Today there had been too many mistakes. There had been the phone call from Jeremy and the mention of flights. Then there had been the look on his face when she had been so close to his stepfather in the study. Did he see the likeness?

Sometimes she saw it herself and if her father had not looked so ill it would have been very apparent. Alex was used to summing things up from looks alone. Hadn't she thought of him as a sort of medical detective? He would need few clues here. One thing was certain. She had to meet her mother on Monday. Things were closing in on her and she hadn't felt so scared for a long, long time.

Just after breakfast the next day, Fiona left. She lingered mournfully around Alex, resting her head against him and showing such a reluctance to let him go that for one dreadful moment Erica thought she would change her mind and come back into the house. The car finally pulled away, though, and Alex came back indoors.

Erica settled down to her painting. As it was Saturday, Alex was home and she felt it necessary to stay in her room for as long as possible. She had been forced to go down for breakfast but both Alex and Fiona had ignored her, and as they had been there it had not been possible to speak to her father about going to London on Monday.

She had intended to wait until she could get him alone but at lunchtime Alex forced things out into the open with a certain amount of malice.

'Has Erica mentioned that she wants the day off on Monday?' he asked when they were seated and Mrs Roberts had left the room. It was a very deliberate action. He strongly suspected that she had said nothing of the sort and he just wanted to see her squirm.

'I haven't had the chance,' Erica said, ignoring him and addressing her words to her father. 'If you can possibly spare me I really would like to go to London on Monday. I'll go by train and make the journey there and back in one day.'

'Of course, Erica!' her father exclaimed. 'You haven't had a day off since you've been here. Come to think of it,' he added in some bewilderment, 'I haven't paid you, either. Why didn't you remind me, my dear? I'm just not used to having anything so grand as a secretary and you fit in here like one of the family. I quite forgot. I'll let you have a cheque right after lunch.'

'It doesn't matter,' Erica assured him. 'All I want is Monday off. As to the other, pay me when I leave.'

'That's unwise,' Alex said darkly. 'He may never let you go.'

'Well, I wish I was writing about a dozen books,' Philip laughed. 'That way I'd get to keep her for a good while longer.'

'The boyfriend would object,' Alex murmured. 'He's kicking his heels in London right now, eagerly awaiting her arrival. Erica is pining for him too. I doubt if you could keep her here.'

He was in a horrid, taunting mood and as soon as her father had finished his lunch Erica fled from the scene. She was beginning to feel very trapped. Enjoying her lovely room was one thing, being forced to hide there was quite another and she put on her thick clothes and went outside as soon as she knew that Alex was securely in his own study.

Her father didn't work on Saturdays and she had no idea what he was doing. She would have liked to find out. She would have liked to talk to him but Alex would have noticed and in his present mood there was no knowing what he would say.

It was snowing again but it was not nearly so cold, and as Erica walked round the back Mrs Roberts opened the back door and let Charlie out.

'Take him with you, dear,' she begged. 'He's getting right under my feet and I'm doing my baking today. What with one thing and another I haven't been able to get on.'

Erica nodded. 'One thing and another' just about described Fiona Croft. She had managed to have Mrs Roberts running all over for her.

Erica whistled for Charlie and he looked round in very glad surprise before running towards her, barking loudly. He could hardly believe his luck and as Erica bent to pat his head her eyes caught a movement at one of the windows. Alex was watching her and she stiffened immediately, turning and walking off at as brisk a pace as she could manage, painfully aware that she was wearing the clothes he had bought for her even though she wasn't speaking to him after last night's episode.

It was a bit like a winter wonderland. Erica crossed the fields and entered the woods at the back of the house. She had never been there before and they sheltered her from the worst of the snow. In any case it was the sort of soft, heavy fall that came straight down. It was not the driving, stinging kind she had encountered during her search for the craft cottage. Charlie began a fruitless search for rabbits and, without really knowing it, Erica went further and further into the woods.

This time coming back was no problem, and by the time she turned round Erica felt quite refreshed. She followed her own tracks and Charlie scurried along before her, his nose taking him to several interesting places on the way. It was very pleasing to find that he accepted her and when he disappeared for a while she practised her whistle and he obeyed instantly.

She was almost at the edge of the wood when Alex appeared, and as he saw her his face changed and he took a deep breath. He had been looking concerned but now he was back to being exasperated.

'I am not lost!' Erica informed him crossly before he could say anything at all. 'I do not need to be followed, checked on or rescued. I am alive and well—'

'And angry with me,' he finished for her as he came up to her and stood in front of her. 'I can see all that for myself.'

'Then why are you here?' she enquired sharply.

'Because I worry about you, damn it!' he snapped. 'I also have the other members of the household on my back nowadays. There's Philip anxiously looking out of the window and making small but significant remarks about the snow. There's Mrs Roberts fluttering about berating herself for asking you to take the dog out from under her feet. I'm supposed to be preparing a paper for tomorrow and in the end I'm joining them in their vigil. We're all looking for Erica, the lost lamb.'

'I'm not lost!' Erica pointed out frustratedly. 'This is quite ridiculous. I've never had anyone worry about me in my whole life and now I can't make a move without explaining myself.'

'It's because you're fascinating.' Alex grunted, turning back and walking beside her. 'Philip needs you. Mrs Roberts dotes on you, and me...'

'And you have to keep an eye on me in case I'm up to no good,' Erica put in.

'I suppose so,' he growled. He suddenly turned, cupping her face in his hands, looking deeply into her eyes.

'Tell me, Erica,' he demanded quietly.

She nearly did then. It was secluded here, safe, beautiful. Nobody would interrupt them. Nobody would hear. And he looked so calm, so dependable, so caring. He would be angry, though, and she would not be able to avoid telling her father if she told Alex.

'There's nothing, Alex,' she managed carefully.

'There is,' he persisted, his hands still cupping her face. 'Whatever it is, it will finally come out. You fit in here so well. You seem to belong here. Just tell me and let's get it out of the way.'

'I can't.' She delicately extricated herself from his hands and turned back to the walk. 'I don't fit in here,' she continued softly. A little smile came to her face, wistful and tremulous. 'I wish I did fit in but it's a very different life from my own. I'll finish the book and then I'll go. Even if I wanted to stay it would be impossible.'

'There's the boyfriend,' Alex surmised harshly, keeping pace with her. 'There's also the mystery.'

'If you think there's a mystery then I suppose I must say yes to both those things,' Erica agreed, and he said nothing more. He walked with her back to the house in complete silence and Erica didn't feel happy after all.

The next day he had gone before she'd got up and when she asked her father where Alex was on a Sunday morning he told her that there was a conference in London.

'It's today and tomorrow,' he said. 'Alex is presenting a paper. He's going to be the main speaker so he could hardly miss it. It think they have lunch and then spend the afternoon there. Apparently there's a dinner tonight and then more conference tomorrow. I don't know much about medical bigwigs but Alex's important.'

Erica knew that. He was too important to have her fluttering at the edge of his life and if she stayed here she would not be just at the edge of it. There was something between them that told her so. When he kissed her he felt what she felt. It was only just beginning to dawn on her exactly how he treated her. He seemed to be unable to remain aloof and she knew it was frustrating him.

She wondered rather mournfully if Fiona would be going to this dinner with the medical bigwigs. Probably. Fiona would fit in well with her expensive clothes and hairdo. If she could just curb her urge to have it all her own way Fiona would fit very well into Alex's life. And Alex cared about her.

CHAPTER SEVEN

THE snowploughs had caught up with the backlog of work by Monday morning and Erica viewed the scene with very few misgivings. She had already stated that she intended to go to London by train and she had every intention of driving to the station and leaving her car there as she caught the train through from Edinburgh to London.

That plan was doomed, however, because her father appeared at breakfast and announced that he had ordered her a taxi.

'I arranged it last night,' he told her firmly. 'It's quite a drive to the nearest station. The London train doesn't stop just anywhere.'

'I could have managed perfectly well,' Erica said, quite touched that he had worried about her. Now that the taxi had been ordered she would have to take it and quite obviously he would be easier in his mind.

'It's safer this way,' Philip assured her. 'Anyway,' he added, as if the matter was settled beyond recall, 'Alex insisted. I didn't see him on Sunday before he set off but he gave me a firm lecture on Saturday night. I was to put you in a taxi.'

'I suppose he drove to the station?' Erica murmured drily. It gave her a funny feeling inside to realise that in spite of the fact that they had not parted on friendly terms Alex had thought about her trip and taken action.

'He's used to these roads,' Philip pointed out. 'He's got a strong, powerful car. Besides, he can take care of himself.'

'So can I,' Erica reminded him, but he shook his head and looked at her sternly.

'Perhaps you can, my dear. We'll take no chances, though. I don't want Mrs Roberts wringing her hands at me and I certainly don't want to face Alex's displeasure when he comes back. He's a very calm man but he can be quite stroppy when the mood takes him. You're to get a taxi back from the station, too. Alex's going to pay for it when he gets back.'

'He is not,' Erica stated sharply. 'I'm not a schoolgirl.'

Her father gave her a quick grin, mischief written all over his face.

'I'm only passing on orders. You can have a battle with Alex later. He didn't look too pleased on Saturday night so I would consider things carefully before you set about him.'

It was something that would have to be left, and right at that moment the thing uppermost in Erica's mind was the meeting with her mother. She rang Jeremy before she set off. It seemed unreasonable to be in London and not even see him.

He had been a friend for a long time and although she knew he would like to take things further Erica was not at all interested. Even if she had been, the old fear would have materialised and she would have been left shattered. It was better to continue the way she had always been.

When the train arrived, Jeremy was waiting for her. Erica had made it quite clear that he would not be able to be with her when she met her mother but he seemed to be content to wait.

'I've nothing particular to do today,' he said quite amiably as he drove her from the station. 'I'll hang around and wait for you. We can have a meal later on.'

'I'm catching the train back to Northumberland,' Erica told him. 'I'm going back tonight.'

'What have you got up there—a secret boyfriend?'

'It's just this job I've taken.'

It was a temptation to correct him and say that she had a secret father, but she would never let that information slip out. She knew she could tell Jeremy and he would be quite intrigued. He might even offer advice but she had such a certainty of Alex's omnipotence that she dared not breathe a word of it. Even thinking about it seemed to be dangerous.

Her mother was waiting and as soon as Erica saw her she knew there would be trouble. It had always been easy to see trouble brewing with her mother, and today her lips were set in a determined way as if she had come to some decision.

During lunch, the interrogation began.

'I know what you're doing up there, Erica,' she said sharply. 'You've found your father and you're staying with him.'

'I've taken a job to help towards a better flat,' Erica contradicted without even looking up from her meal. 'It came at just the right moment.'

'You mean just as he was doing a book?' There was a scathing sound to her mother's voice that told Erica she was quite certain of her facts. 'I have my sources,' she went on with a grim smile. 'I suppose I followed the same trail you followed yourself. The only difference was that I got somebody to do it for me. I still have contacts in television.'

It was useless to prevaricate and Erica looked at her levelly.

'Keep out of it, Mother. You're not married to him now. It's years since you had anything to do with him. I just wanted to see him.'

'And what does he think of his daughter?' Her mother looked at her with tightened lips. 'I'm surprised the shock didn't kill him.'

'I didn't tell him and I have no intention of telling him,' Erica stated. 'He's not very well. He doesn't need shocks. He doesn't need a daughter either. His life is too set for any interference. He's a very nice man.'

'Nicer than your father, you mean?' her mother snapped, and Erica snapped back immediately.

'He *is* my father. I've only ever had one father and now I've found him. Leave me to enjoy his company while I can. When I've finished the work I probably won't see him again ever. If I can leave as a friend and maybe write to him as a friend that's all I want.'

'And that's all Jack wants! He never sees you. He brought you up and cared for you when Philip Macbride just deserted you and now all the thanks Jack gets is that you refuse to even call at home and never even send him a card.'

'I'm living my own life,' Erica pointed out stiffly. The urge to face her mother with the real facts was very strong but she had kept silent for years and the silence won. 'When this is over, I'll be flying out to all parts. I never have any time.'

'Excuses!' her mother accused her sharply. 'Look at us now, meeting like mere acquaintances!'

'*You* married Jack Linton!' Erica was stung to reply hotly. 'It wasn't my idea.'

'So you wanted me to be alone all my life? Just the sort of thanks I would expect from you.'

'I'm going.' Erica stood, leaving the rest of her meal. 'If this is all I came down here for then I could have saved myself the trouble.'

'Oh, it's not all.' Her mother looked up at her angrily. 'I've put up with you asking about your real father for years, ignoring the father who raised you. This is just the last straw, Erica. I intend to do something about it.'

'Don't you dare intrude in my life!' Erica commanded, leaning forward to emphasise the words. 'If you have any ideas about coming up to Northumberland...'

'I haven't decided exactly what to do yet,' her mother informed her. She sat back and smiled quite smugly, seeing very well that she had Erica in a turmoil. 'I have to give it some more thought.'

'Don't make me hate you, Mother,' Erica warned, and her mother looked at her with narrowed eyes.

'Like you hate Jack, you mean?' she asked coldly.

'Yes!' Erica spat out. 'Yes, I hate him, and if you had any sense at all you would ask yourself why.'

She just walked out, and as she got to the door Jeremy stood up from another table and joined her.

'What are you doing here?' she asked angrily, not even looking at him but making her way to the street with sharp steps.

'I had to eat. Eating in the same place was the best thing to do. That way I could be ready when you left. I didn't exactly think you'd leave so soon. My lunch was good. Unfortunately I had to abandon half of it.'

'I'm sorry,' Erica muttered. 'But I never asked you to—'

'How about a drink and a sandwich?' he proposed quietly. 'You look as if you need the drink, and you left most of your meal too. You can tell me your problems.'

'I'll never tell a soul for the whole of my life,' Erica said bitterly. 'I'm quite used to dealing with things by myself. You're a good friend, Jeremy, but don't pry.'

'Or I'll get the boot?' he queried with a wry grin.

'That just about covers the situation.' She looked up at him and laughed. 'Let's have that drink. You can tell me about your flight.'

'Safe ground,' he sighed, taking her arm and steering her across to his car. 'First, we'll leave the immediate area. I would not want your mother to encounter us and start again.'

'Could you hear?' Erica spun round and looked at him with a certain amount of anxiety but he shook his head, reassuring her.

'I could see her face. She was out for trouble, but then, I knew that when I phoned you.'

'Well, thanks for phoning me,' Erica murmured.

There was no doubt that her mother had been out for trouble. Just how much trouble she was prepared to make was another matter. Erica was not sure if she had warned her off sufficiently but it had not been possible to say any more. Maybe it would turn out to be too much of a task to interfere. Her mother had never liked to be disturbed in her very set life. It all depended on how far the vindictive need to hurt Philip went.

Later, Jeremy took her back to the station and walked with her to the train.

'Not very satisfying,' he murmured drily. 'Just get back to work soon, Erica. I see a lot more of you when we're on the same flight.'

'I'll be back.' She turned and smiled up at him. 'I may very well be back sooner than expected. Anyway, there's not much of the month left.'

'I'm pleased to hear it. Meanwhile, don't go getting too cold up there.'

'Oh, I won't!' Erica assured him brightly and quite thoughtlessly. 'Alex bought me some thick clothes.'

She stopped abruptly as Jeremy's eyebrows shot up but it was a little too late.

'And who is Alex?' he asked with a frown. 'Close enough to be allowed to buy you things, it seems. I remember getting a very cold glance for buying you a swimsuit.'

'Oh, it's not like that,' Erica murmured quickly. 'He's the—the doctor.'

'It must be very cosy up there. Down here doctors prescribe medicine. They don't buy patients clothes.'

'He's a friend of my employer,' Erica improvised speedily. 'I have to humour him. He—er—he's old.'

Jeremy gave her a sceptical look and then decided to see the funny side of things.

'Watch him,' he warned. 'The old ones are the worst.' He grinned down at her and then reached forward and gave her a warm hug. 'Ring me,' he begged. 'I have another two days.' He drew back and looked at her closely. 'Don't let your mother spoil things for you, Erica. I know it's none of my business but she had a very mean look about her.'

Erica nodded. She knew that. It did not bode well for the rest of her stay at Keresford House. Still, as she had told Jeremy, the time was rapidly drawing to an end. She gave a small sigh of regret and was quite touched and surprised when Jeremy kissed her gently.

'Cheer up,' he ordered. 'Don't let things get you down and hurry back to your mates. We all miss you.'

Erica smiled and turned to the train. It was full and she was not looking forward to spending the journey crushed up with strangers. She glanced wryly at the first-class section, knowing it would be half-empty, and then she almost gasped in shock.

Alex was there. He was looking out of the window, watching her, and his face looked as cold as the landscape he lived in. He had seen her parting with Jeremy and his mind would be working like a well-oiled machine, adding this latest information to his store of facts and suspicions. All she could be grateful for was that he had not seen her with her mother.

It was very dark and cold when she got off the train after the journey and Erica hurried along, trying to get to a taxi before Alex spotted her. Unfortunately there were few people leaving the train—most passengers were going on to Edinburgh—and as she came out of the station the voice she had been expecting halted her in her tracks.

'Erica!'

There was a deep authority in the sound and she would not have had the nerve to ignore it even if she had not been going to be forced to face him back at the house. She stopped, drawing her coat closely around her to cut out the cold wind that blew along the platform.

He had been to a conference, she knew, and she was not surprised to see that he was dressed accordingly. He looked tall, handsome and intimidating.

'You know perfectly well that I'll drive you home,' he pointed out irascibly. 'Why are you hurrying off? You saw me on the train.'

'I wasn't sure if you'd seen me,' Erica hedged. 'You didn't smile or anything.'

'I was looking straight at you. As to smiling, I didn't feel like it. All of which is neither here nor there,' he continued. 'You knew I was on the train. Waiting for me would have been the normal thing to do.'

'Maybe I'm not normal.' Erica shivered. 'Can we go now? If you want to shout at me you could do it when we get back. It's cold here.'

'I'm not in the habit of shouting, even with you,' Alex muttered, taking her arm and striding off. 'Shaking you sometimes sneaks into my mind but so far I've restrained myself.'

'I'd sue you for assault,' Erica threatened, trotting to keep up with him. 'You have nothing to do with me.'

'And I sometimes wish that were true,' Alex growled, tightening his grasp.

'I'll be gone soon,' she said quietly, and his hand tightened even more.

'You've not finished typing the manuscript, nor have you finished the painting. Leaving Philip halfway through is not a possibility.'

He opened the car and ushered her inside and as he came round to sit beside her Erica turned to him urgently.

'Don't try to blackmail me. I came for one month and it's nearly up. It was the agreed time and the only time I could spare.'

'Really?' He started the car and turned out of the station yard and onto the road. 'As I recall, you're at a loose end, trying to decide what to do next. You even considered going overseas but there was nothing suitable. It therefore seems to me that you have plenty of time to spare—certainly enough to see this thing out with Philip.'

She would have agreed, been delighted but now there was another consideration to take into account. How long could she hope to keep her mother at bay? How long before her mother decided either to come up here or do something else about her ex-husband?

'I can't stay,' she said stubbornly. 'I *won't* stay!'

'Then I'll just have to speed up my investigations,' Alex murmured. 'I'm another step forward. Today I saw the boyfriend.'

Erica kept very quiet. It seemed that anything she said would be noted and remembered and all she could hope for was a quick end to her time here in Northumberland.

'Was it the boyfriend?' he persisted, and Erica had to reply or look childishly foolish.

'Obviously,' she muttered. 'You were watching. I imagine you saw him kiss me goodbye. It should have been quite plain that he was my boyfriend.'

'Why?' Alex asked drily. 'I've kissed you a good deal more thoroughly than the chaste little salute he gave you.'

'He—he has every right to kiss me. You haven't,' Erica pointed out unevenly, and he laughed, his dark eyes slanting a glance of amusement at her.

'How disappointing,' he taunted. 'I really was beginning to feel I had every right in the world.'

She went silent again. She sometimes thought that too. It was only when she came to her senses that she remembered who he was and who she was. The house, the surroundings, her father and Alex seemed to have a drugging effect on her. It was only when she had been away as she had today that she knew how foolish she was to allow herself to be drawn into their lives.

It was a long drive and in spite of her anxieties the day caught up with Erica. The car was warm, smoothly driven and the snow-covered countryside was dark, lulling her to sleep. It had been a wearing day and she was troubled by the threat her mother had made. She was also troubled by the great leap of excitement she had felt when she had seen Alex on the train. She was fast allowing herself to sink into an impossible situation.

She moved down in the comfortable seat and closed her eyes, letting everything drift away. After a while, her head slid to Alex's shoulder and he glanced down at her with a wry smile. He frowned and looked back at the road. For some reason she looked worn out, as much on edge as she had been when she had first come here.

His eyes narrowed thoughtfully. Sometimes she looked like a little lost soul and his desire to protect her was overwhelming. Sometimes she was just secretive. Now she seemed to be both at once. From the first he had been convinced that she was here for some purpose. Now he was sure it had something to do with Philip. Somehow he must find out before she left. The last thought brought a black frown to his face and he drove on grimly, not at all surprised when it began to snow again.

Erica awoke next day feeling uneasy and worried. Since she had settled into the house she had relaxed more and more but now the old feelings pushed at her mind. Too many memories, too much bitterness—and her mother was about to force things out into the open.

It wouldn't happen. She could not let it happen. At least she would leave here with her new-found friendship with her father intact. That would not be possible if her mother managed to reveal all her subterfuge. He would never trust her again and Alex would look at her with disgust.

Last night she had been asleep when they had arrived at the house and Alex had wakened her very gently. For a minute he hadn't seemed to be annoyed any more. Her father had greeted her with relief too, as if he had been looking forward to her coming back. It had been like coming home, and in her sleepy state she had gone to bed and dreamed that Alex rescued her from a terrible danger and held her fast in his arms, telling her it was all right.

It was not all right. She dressed and went downstairs, only to find that Alex had gone early and that her father was not up yet.

'He's not too well today,' Mrs Roberts told her solemnly. 'My goodness, I hope he's not going to have one of his attacks but Miss Fiona always upsets him, and without you here yesterday he couldn't settle.'

Erica didn't know what to do. She wanted to go to his room and see how he was but that was out of the question. She had no rights at all. She went to the study and started her typing but in reality her mind was not on it. She was constantly thinking of her father upstairs, wondering how he was.

Just before lunch, Mrs Roberts came in to remind her that it was her day for the market.

'There's just the one bus there and just one back,' she said briskly. 'I have to leave now. I've put your lunch on the table and covered it. There's some soup for Mr Macbride. Can you take it up for me, dear? If I stay to take it up myself the bus will be gone.'

Erica was glad to agree. It was the excuse she had been waiting for and as Mrs Roberts left she hurried into the kitchen to warm up the soup and set the tray for her father. She wasn't sure which room he had but it was one along the passage towards the end. It would be easy to find it.

When she finally located the room there was no reply to her knock, and after hesitating for a while Erica went quietly in. At first she couldn't see where he was. The room was dark, the curtains still drawn and she knew that Mrs Roberts had been too intent on her market day to come up here at all this morning.

She could see at last that he was in bed and when she went over to take a closer look Erica felt a wave of fear. Even in the dim light he looked terrible and she quickly put down the tray and pulled the curtains back to take a closer look. He was lying too still. Perspiration had trickled onto his face and neck and it was easy to see that at some time he had been tossing restlessly in bed.

Now, though, there was no movement at all and at first Erica thought he was not breathing. He was burning when she touched him but he didn't move. For a second she stood there petrified. She was alone in the house and she had no idea what to do. Her only thought was, Alex! It was like a great, lost cry in her mind and she ran from the room and flew down the stairs.

There was a book in the hall on the table and as she looked she saw that it was a telephone book, a neat, covered book where private numbers were kept. She just prayed that Alex's hospital number was there.

It was but when she got through there was a rather shocked silence when she asked to speak to him.

'This is urgent!' Erica said loudly. 'I *must* speak to him!'

'He's seeing patients by appointment this morning. I'll put you through to his private secretary but I doubt if he'll have the time—'

'He will!' Erica insisted, and she stood there agitatedly as the call was switched.

It seemed like ages before she could convince the woman who answered that this was important, and she only managed it when she said that there was an emergency at his own home.

Relief just raced through her as she heard his calm, deep voice.

'Alex Thorne,' he announced quietly, and she knew that no message had been passed at all. He had no idea who she was.

'Alex!' she began urgently. 'You've got to come back. You've got to!'

'Erica?' He heard her agitation and was alert at once. 'What is it? Calm down and just tell me.'

'It's Philip—Mr Macbride. He's lying so still and he's burning hot. I can't make him wake up. He's breathing so strangely. Mrs Roberts is out. Please, Alex! What shall I do?'

'I'll be back as soon as I can get there,' he assured her quickly. 'Meanwhile, keep him well wrapped up and sponge his forehead and face with cool water. It's all right. I've seen him like this before.'

'Will he die?'

'No, Erica,' he said softly. 'When I get back, we'll deal with him, you and I. He may have to go into hospital but with any luck we can cope without that. Now do what you can until I get there.'

'Yes,' she whispered, and his voice became deeper still, soothing and quiet.

'I'll be there soon, as fast as I can. Just do exactly what I've told you.'

'I will,' she promised, and then added with another burst of agitation, 'Alex! Drive carefully.'

He put the phone down and she ran to the kitchen, searching for something to carry the water to her father's room. She had a face-cloth in her own room and she hurried back upstairs, dreading what she would find when she finally opened the door and went across to the bed.

He was just the same and she tucked the blankets closely around him, covering him as much as possible before she started to bathe his head and face. He looked so bad and she dreaded that she would lose him when she had found him after so long. She told herself that Alex would be here soon and the thought calmed her. He would take charge. He would always know what to do.

It was a long time before she heard Alex's car arrive and even then Erica dared not go to meet him. It seemed to her that her ministrations had been useless. Her father looked as bad as ever and when Alex walked into the room she turned to him with dismay on her face.

'Let me see.' He took her shoulders and moved her aside and the responsibility was gone at once. He was a doctor, somebody she didn't quite know.

She was mesmerised by the sight of the long, strong fingers, the utter calm of every action, and her own agitation seemed to ease as Alex examined his patient.

'What is it?' she whispered. 'Nobody ever told me what—'

'Malaria,' Alex muttered, his mind not on her question at all. 'I think we'll have him in hospital for a few days.'

'I thought you could prevent malaria?' In a way it was a relief to hear the word, to know it was not something worse, but she could see how ill her father was.

'If you take all the necessary precautions,' Alex said, standing and looking down at her father with a thoughtful frown. 'At some time in the past, Philip forgot, or maybe he was too involved with his animals

to bother. He got a particularly virulent strain and the
attacks recur. They can recur for years. It causes anaemia
and, as in Philip's case, affects the liver.'

'But—but it won't kill him?'

'No. It's just debilitating.' He turned away and muttered, 'I should have seen this coming last night. I was
too busy thinking about you.'

He was walking to the door and Erica looked at him
woefully.

'So, you're saying it's my fault?'

'Of course I'm not!' he snapped at her, and then he
turned back, smiling ruefully. 'I'm the doctor, Erica.
It's my business to notice. Unfortunately, I'm human
too and you occupy my mind when I should be thinking
about other things.'

That wasn't a great deal of help. She knew he was
thinking about her with a good deal of suspicion. It must
be difficult to be a doctor and a private investigator at
the same time.

'Can you pack him a few things?' Alex asked quietly.
'I'll get in touch with the hospital. We're going to need
an ambulance. He's very weak.'

Erica nodded, biting at her lip anxiously, and as Alex
left the room she looked round with some misgivings.
It seemed impertinent to look into her father's things.
Still, somebody had to do it, and if she had been here
it would undoubtedly have been Mrs Roberts. At least
it meant that she could do something for him.

When the ambulance had come and gone, Erica faced
Alex a little desperately.

'Can I go to the hospital?' She knew perfectly well
that she was simply asking for more suspicion with this
request. After all, she was supposed to be a secretary,
and not a secretary of long-standing at that. This

eagerness to be with her employer could only make Alex
look at her more closely. She was not happy about staying
away, though, and it was a risk she was prepared to take.

'No, I don't think so,' Alex said firmly, and when she
turned away without another word he reached out and
turned her back impatiently. 'For heaven's sake, Erica!'
he growled. 'I'm not trying to cut you out of this. It's
a matter of logistics. If I take you through with me now,
you may well be stuck there for hours. Once I get into
that hospital there'll be people who would have managed
very well without me who suddenly feel the urgent need
for my advice. I can't just tell them to get lost. I'll have
to stay and deal with whatever comes up.'

'I can take my own car. I can drive myself there and
back,' Erica pointed out, but he looked more frustrated
than ever.

'Please don't,' he said wearily. 'We never know what
the weather is going to do up here and we're still in a
bad spell of snow. There's Philip and there'll be at least
half a dozen other people plucking at my sleeve when I
get there. Just leave me one little corner of peace. Let
me know that you'll be warm and safe here.'

'All right.' Erica felt an unusual surge of emotion that
brought a slight, wistful smile to her lips. 'I'm capable
of taking care of myself, though. I always have taken
care of myself.'

'I don't want you to take care of yourself,' Alex said
with a sudden harsh note to his voice. 'While you're not
taking care of yourself, I'm worrying about you.'

'It's all right,' Erica managed unevenly, giving in and
looking quickly away from the dark eyes as her cheeks
began to flush with colour. His intent gaze was making
her heart pound and she wanted to escape now. 'I'll stay

re if it will make you easier in your mind. I don't want
bother you.'

'But you do bother me, Erica,' Alex murmured. He
ached out and pulled her closer, wrapping strong arms
ound her. 'You've bothered me since I first saw you.'
e tilted her face, forcing her to meet his eyes. 'I bother
ou too—when you're not being overwhelmed and scared
y my so-called importance.'

His eyes moved to her lips and Erica felt the deep
embling start inside.

'Shouldn't you be going now?' she whispered. 'You
ave to see to my—to Mr Macbride.'

'Yes, I should.' His head slowly bent as he moved in-
ntly to her lips. 'Were you going to call him your em-
loyer again, Erica? Or was that almost a slip of greater
anger?'

'Please, Alex!' She pressed her hands uselessly against
is chest but his soft laughter was almost breathed into
er mouth.

'I'll go when you've warmed me up for the journey,'
e told her huskily, and his lips closed over hers.

It was utterly silent in the house and Alex had already
sed away her fears and any sort of fight that this situ-
tion would normally have brought. When he gathered
er closer, Erica didn't even try to resist. He was quite
onderful to her and she knew it. She looked upon him
s some towering being way beyond her comprehension.
er lips softened and her slender arms linked willingly
ehind his neck as she accepted the kiss gladly.

'I don't want homage,' Alex breathed against her lips.
want you just as you really are, with all the fight and
ll the temper. No pretending, Erica.'

'Do you always know what I'm thinking?' Erica asked
reamily. Her head fell back and his lips moved hungrily

over her neck before returning to her flushed cheeks a
her lips.

'Not always. Not nearly enough. I know I have to
careful or you'll panic but I know too that you're ve
close to taking the risk of caring about me.'

'I—I do care about you,' Erica admitted tremulous
and he caught her mouth with his, kissing her ling
ingly before he let her go.

'One day you're going to have to prove that,' he sa
deeply. He turned to the door and she couldn't let hi
go just like that.

'Will you ring me?' she asked breathlessly.

'No. I'll tell you all there is to know when I co
back.' He suddenly turned and smiled at her. 'You'll ha
to deal with Mrs Roberts yourself. Maybe I've got t
easiest job after all. She'll panic.'

'Then I'll just tell her he's gone for a check-up,' Eri
stated, and his eyes were intent again as he stared at h

'Which will not be exactly true. Do you find it ea
to sidestep the truth, Erica?'

'When it's very necessary,' she muttered, avoiding
eyes. 'Sometimes it's better for—for everybody.'

'Perhaps.' He looked at her for another second a
then left, but he was no longer smiling, and Erica sto
for a long time and tried to gather her trembling feelin
together. She felt as if she had known him her wh
life. The idea of never seeing him again was beginni
to hurt more than a little. He was safety, comfort a
excitement. Alex had been allowed to be closer to
than anyone she had ever known. She didn't panic w
him.

He seemed to know her well enough to feel
emotions. He expected fright but he would never kn
how much fright there could be. With him, it just did

surface. Her main fear had become the thought that he would discover her secret and be disgusted with her. She did care about him. She cared what he thought of her and she needed the right to be close to him.

Erica sighed and went upstairs to tidy her father's room—another right she did not really have. How would she remember her stay here when she had to go? She didn't even like to consider it because she wanted to be here always. It was not possible. Staying here and continuing the subterfuge would not be enough and she knew it. There was also the matter of her mother. One day, her mother would take some action. It might be very soon.

CHAPTER EIGHT

WAITING for Alex proved to be very difficult. In spite of his assurances, Erica felt sure that her father was in danger. She knew nothing about malaria but she did know he had been unconscious. She had seen his feverish look and it had frightened her more than she would have believed possible.

She felt as close to him as if he had never been away in her life. It might have been just some primitive instinct but the feeling was too strong to ignore. For the most part she spent her time simply pacing about, waiting in case Alex should change his mind and ring her.

When Mrs Roberts came back from the market Erica had the tricky job of giving her the latest news without alarming her and she approached the task very methodically, pushing aside her own feelings. Not that it did much good.

There were floods of tears, self-recriminations and great gloomy forebodings for the future. In the end, Erica had to take some positive action, if only to put an end to the dire tales of woe that were only making her feel worse herself.

'There was a man in the village like that.' Mrs Roberts sniffed, drying her eyes. Even the movement of her hands was melancholy and Erica could not really back out of the kitchen without looking extremely hard and uncaring.

'A man with malaria?' Erica queried, knowing the unlikeliness of that and preparing to explain the lack of similarity. She was too worried herself to listen to this.

'It probably was,' Mrs Roberts surmised in a chilling whisper.

'Had he lived overseas in any of the known malaria places?' Erica pressed with growing impatience.

'He probably had.' Mrs Roberts looked at her with desperation. 'He died!' She burst into tears again and Erica made her mind up about instant action. Promise to Alex or not, this had to stop.

'I'm taking his things to the hospital,' she said briskly. 'When I get back I'll give you all the latest news. Now just carry on as normal and it will take your mind off things.'

'You're a sensible girl,' Mrs Roberts complimented her in a watery voice. 'Miss Fiona wouldn't have bothered at all. She wouldn't have gone out on a day like this. She's not kind like you.'

Fiona didn't need to be kind, Erica mused dismally as she packed the things she had sorted out for the hospital. Fiona had it made. She just had to wait around looking beautiful and Alex would marry her. She would make a good wife for a consultant. She would always be immaculate and prepared, the sort of person Alex could take to some big dinner with no qualms.

There were no nasty skeletons lurking around behind Fiona. There would be no past to catch up with her. Erica picked up the bag and went downstairs with a tight look on her face. Whatever she did, it would be the wrong thing. If she stayed here, Mrs Roberts would not stop at all and by the time Alex came back they would *both* be hysterical.

Going to the hospital was directly disobeying Alex's orders and if he saw her he would be furious. Any course of action would bring problems so she might just as well follow her inclinations. Every inclination was to see her father so she would just have to sneak in and hope for the best. One thing was good. It was not snowing and the forecast had been very hopeful. Frost but no snow. Not that it mattered. She was committed to going, whatever the weather did.

She made her way back to the motorway. The roadworks were finished in the narrow road and it was with some relief that Erica joined the motorway and found it clear of both snow and traffic. The directions that Mrs Roberts had given her were simple enough and she had no problem at all.

It was only as she parked at the hospital that Erica experienced renewed qualms about this action. For the very first time she was stepping into Alex's domain and she felt very insignificant and sneaky. As she walked to the main doors she had to pass the private parking facilities for staff and her eyes were drawn anxiously to the place marked 'Consultants'. Alex's car was there. It looked expensive and important, parked in its own special place, and Erica eyed it warily. She would have to do a lot of darting about to remain undetected.

She was directed to the ward where her father was and once there it was easy enough to bluff it out. She had to do this fast but she certainly had to do it or the trip and the disobedience would have been for nothing at all.

'I've brought some personal things for Mr Macbride,' she announced firmly when the nurse on duty came to speak to her. 'He was admitted not long ago. I'm his secretary.'

For a minute her spirits rose. She felt as her father must have felt when he had realised his importance in having a secretary. The title seemed to give her prestige, and she stood very straight and businesslike.

'If I could just take them in to him...?' she murmured, as if it was very obviously necessary.

'I'm sure it will be all right,' the nurse said pleasantly. 'He's Dr Thorne's stepfather after all. Nobody would like to upset Dr Thorne. He's wonderful.'

Erica's heart sank one notch very quickly, her feeling of importance vanishing. Here was another woman who swooned over Alex. She looked pretty too. The nurses would all be throwing themselves at his feet and they would be with him every day. Doctors often married nurses. She had read that somewhere. She followed the nurse along the quiet corridor, gloomily comparing her own position with that of the women here. She had never done such a thing before in her life and every small comparison left her more isolated, more distant from Alex.

'In here.' The nurse stood aside and smiled at her. 'Mr Macbride came round but he's sleeping now. He's a lot better. You can put his things in the locker and I'll tell him later. No harm in having a glance at him while you're here.'

'Is he all right?' Erica asked, feeling grateful for this kindness and ashamed of her gloomy, jealous thoughts.

'He's not in any danger, if that's what you mean,' the nurse assured her brightly. 'He has these attacks but bit by bit he'll get better. You'll have to leave in a second or two,' she added with a quick glance up the corridor. 'It's not visiting and if Dr Thorne catches me...'

'I'll hurry,' Erica said hastily. If Dr Thorne caught anyone it would be her. The nurse might get a sharp reprimand but when he came home *she* would get a long lecture and a hard, dark-eyed stare.

It was a small side-room and her father was lying as still as he had been in the house. Now, though, he looked more rested. He didn't have the alarmingly feverish look about him and she assumed he had been given some sort of sedative. He looked safe and Erica breathed a sigh of relief as she quickly packed his things away.

She lingered for a moment by the bed, her hand covering the rather frail fingers that rested on top of the sheets. He was her father but she didn't even have the right to touch his hand. He had to be lying in a drugged sleep before she dared allow herself that small luxury. What would he think if he knew about her? Would he be embarrassed, annoyed? He would certainly be shocked at her original intention to spy on him and then confront him. Looking back now, it seemed impossible that she had ever had such plans.

The longing to stay there until he opened his eyes was quite overwhelming but she remembered the nurse's warning, and in any case she had to escape now before Alex appeared. She had no idea where he was. He would be caring for her father himself and he could walk in at any moment. She walked out quickly, nodding her thanks to the nurse at the desk and hurrying round the corner to the next corridor, which led to the entrance and safety.

As she turned the corner the whole corridor in front of her was filled with people, and all of them doctors by the look of it. They were young, all with stethoscopes round their necks in a manner that told her it was not yet a comfortable habit. The only comfortable person there was walking in front, the others scurrying behind him like disciples. He was taller, more powerful in build, devastatingly handsome in a grey suit and white shirt and the dark eyes were narrowed on her instantly with anger growing by the second.

'Go on to the ward,' Alex ordered as the whole crowd slowed to match his steps. They seemed to be too much in awe to pass him but Erica wished they would rush madly on and give her time to escape. 'I'll join you in a minute,' he insisted, giving them all a very definite look of dismissal.

They obeyed to a man, glancing curiously at her as they passed, and then there was no hiding because once again the corridor was silent, empty, except for Erica and the man who stood watching her with a very black frown.

'I was under the impression we had an agreement,' he said with icy annoyance when she just stood there and looked at him guiltily. 'I even felt that you gave your word not to venture out of the house.'

'I—I couldn't keep the promise. I had to come here.'

'Why?' he asked with rising anger. 'You imagine I'll neglect your *employer* while you're not watching over him?'

'You know I don't think that!' Erica protested, and his face tightened even more.

'Do I? I only know what you care to tell me and that's not so damned much. I asked you not to come and I explained why. Now you're here as if I'd never even mentioned it.'

'Mrs Roberts burst into tears,' Erica explained lamely. Now that she was telling him, it didn't really sound like a good excuse. 'You've no idea how she went on. I—I had to come to put her out of her misery. If I hadn't—'

'Don't insult my intelligence, Erica!' he rasped. 'You're more than capable of coping with Mrs Roberts. You came because you wanted to see Philip.' His eyes moved over her scathingly. 'Your attachment to him would be quite touching—if it were not unnatural.'

'It's not unnatural!' Erica exclaimed, looking at him reproachfully. 'You just don't understand.'

'And I never will until you tell me,' Alex pointed out angrily. He looked at his watch, the very movement of his arm one of impatience. 'I have to catch up with the

work I left when you called me back to the house. There's
no way I can leave again.'

'I wouldn't have called you back if I hadn't needed
you,' Erica muttered in a voice that was almost tearful
with frustration. 'I suppose you think I should have
coped with that problem too?'

He chose to ignore that remark and stood looking at
her intently for a second.

'You could wait here for me until I leave for home,'
he suggested. It sounded grudging, coldly indifferent and
he hadn't said one word about her father. Erica flew
into a rage.

She hadn't heard him offer a single word of warning
to Fiona when she had set off into the snowy landscape
on her way back to London. Fiona hadn't been forced
to go in a taxi and forced to come back to the house
under Alex's wing. He counted Fiona as a woman. He
counted her as an idiot.

'I have no desire to wait for you,' she snapped. 'I called
you back to the house because I needed your assistance
as a doctor. I don't need you now. I'm not a child and
if you require someone to order about, do it with Fiona.
She doesn't have to be watched as if she's an idiot and
neither do I. You have nothing to do with me at all and
if I want to visit my sick employer—I will!'

'Very well, Miss Linton,' he said coldly, but before he
could say more Erica snapped out at him again.

'Don't call me that!' she raged frustratedly.

'Why? It's your name. Or is that another lie?'

Erica stormed off down the corridor, snatching herself
away from the hand that had come to restrain her. It
wasn't her name, not really. It was a name she had never
wanted, a name she had been forced into. Jack Linton
was not her father and although she might have been

legally adopted her own father had never had a say in the matter.

Her temper carried her to her car and it was only as she was once again on the motorway that Erica came to her senses and reminded herself that she had to face Alex later. Even if he came home at midnight, there was tomorrow. She could hear her own angry words about Fiona and she knew that yet again her raging had been jealousy. She prayed that Alex had not heard it too.

When she had told him not to call her Miss Linton she had been protesting at his formality when she wanted so badly to be close to him. It had neatly left her in a trap—a trap he had probably not even been preparing. She was her own worst enemy as far as Alex was concerned and now there was a very real upsurge of animosity.

This had to be over soon. Maybe she should go before her father came back from hospital. It would be the most sensible thing to do. The trouble was that she didn't want to face the prospect of not seeing him again. She couldn't face the idea of never seeing Alex again either, however angry he was. She wanted to be with him and although it was an impossible dream it was too strong to be ignored.

Settling Mrs Roberts was not difficult. When she knew that Erica had actually seen Philip she breathed a great sigh of relief.

'Oh, you're a sensible girl,' she said comfortably. 'I can trust you completely. I'll be able to sleep tonight now.'

Erica made a wry face as Mrs Roberts went off to the kitchen. Of all the people to trust, she was the worst. She was living a lie here and the lie would stay on even after she had gone. It was not possible to extricate herself from the position at all. Disappearing was the only solution. All the same, she had seen her father, got to know him. She cared for him as if she had known him all her life. Love seemed to be instinctive.

She loved Alex too. It was not easy to admit it because there was little point in it but at least she had learned to trust a man. When she left here she would never see him again but he would be in her mind, a shining, unattainable hero, quiet, amusing and strong.

When Mrs Roberts had gone to her cottage and she went up to bed, Erica sat and looked at herself in the mirror. She had changed here. The sharp, brittle person who had come here for vengeance had totally vanished because someone cared about her.

Her father cared, even though he did not know who she was. In a way, too, Alex cared. He rescued her, helped her and did many small things to make her comfortable. If that was all she ever had, then she was lucky.

Erica showered and got ready for bed, a wistful kind of happiness showing on her face. Maybe she really was an idiot but it didn't feel so bad.

Lying in bed, she found herself once again listening for Alex's car. It was only ten o'clock and she had not really intended to retire so early. There was a touch of cowardice about it because she knew perfectly well that she had come to bed so that she would not have to face Alex when he came home. He would have eaten at the hospital again. Sometimes his hours were far too long. He would be tired, and he would be irritated too, if he thought about her visit to see her father.

Erica got up and put on the light. Her conscience was having a fabulous time digging small knives into her, driving her into real gloom. She had had no right to speak to Alex like that, especially when his orders had been for her own safety. He had asked her to stay at home so that he could have some peace of mind about her and she had disobeyed him and then flown at him when he had remonstrated with her. She hadn't been fair and she knew it. When she finally heard his car arrive, Erica put on her dressing gown and went down to apologise.

Alex was already walking through into the small sitting room as she came down the stairs and he didn't see her. He looked rather alarming and for a second Erica considered retreat. Her need to make some attempt to set things right was too strong, however, and she summoned up her courage and went after him.

He certainly didn't hear her—she had not stopped even to put anything on her feet—but by some odd instinct he seemed to sense her presence.

'Philip is perfectly all right,' he said wearily, without even turning. 'He'll stay there for a couple of days and then he can come back. You may like to know that when he woke up he asked about you.'

'Thank you for telling me,' Erica managed evenly. It was more than a little disconcerting that he made no attempt to turn and face her and she assumed it was annoyance that was keeping him from being in any way affable.

He took off his jacket and tossed it onto a chair and when he finally turned he was loosening his tie, unfastening the top button of his shirt. At least it reduced him to human status, and Erica stood her ground.

'I didn't come to ask about Mr Macbride,' she confessed quietly. It was becoming more and more difficult to remember to call her father that and she took a steadying breath before continuing, 'I came to apologise. I had no right to speak to you as I did at the hospital. I—I also had no valid reason for going there.'

'You took his things in for him. He's grateful,' Alex remarked, dropping to a big easy chair and pinning her

with his dark eyes. He looked so tired that she wanted
to do something for him but he was making this very
awkward.

'I'm glad,' Erica muttered. She looked down, curling
her toes into the softness of the carpet. 'I mean—I'm
glad he wanted them,' she corrected herself hastily,
looking up. 'I don't mean I'm glad about going to the
hospital and speaking to you as I did...' He just went
on looking at her and she bit at her lip worriedly. 'Can
I get you anything?'

'I ate at the hospital,' Alex said briefly, and she knew
she had to get out of there while she could. It made her
embarrassed to be standing there like a child and it was
obvious that Alex was not about to bend at all. She had
managed to make him angry enough to be really cold.

'Right. I—er— Goodnight, then.'

She turned to the door, uncomfortably aware that he
was watching her bleakly, and when he spoke she almost
jumped.

'If you want to do something for me then don't go
running off to hide in your room,' he said quietly, and
Erica turned to look at him, not at all surprised to see
that she was still getting that chill look.

'Do you want a drink or something? A cup of tea?'

'I want you to come here,' Alex murmured, his dark
eyes narrowed on her rather wary face. 'It's time you
and I sorted out a problem.'

Erica advanced slowly. She knew what the problem
was. He was going to start questioning her again and
there was nothing she could say that would make him
less suspicious. Leaving right then would have been a
good idea but after her performance this afternoon she
knew that any hasty retreat would annoy him even more.

'What is it?' Erica stood in front of him looking anxious and he reached forward and caught her wrist in one firm hand.

'I suppose I'm a little disgruntled about the time and effort you spend on making sure that Philip is all right. I know I asked you to keep an eye on him but sometimes you seem to be doing it much too well. I think I'm being petulant and sulky, although I'm not going to admit it.' His eyes roamed slowly over her face. 'Sometimes, I need comfort myself, and there's nobody at all to comfort me.'

He was watching her intently, his hand slowly pulling her towards him, and Erica's heart took off at an alarming rate.

'Fiona,' she gasped desperately. 'If you want comfort, then, Fiona—'

'Won't do at all,' Alex said softly. 'Fiona is about as comfortable as a pincushion. I want you to comfort me, Erica. You usually manage it without even trying.'

He pulled her down onto his lap and Erica looked up at him with a sort of hopeless acknowledgement of destiny.

'It's all right.' He smiled into her eyes and pulled her close, settling her against his shoulder. 'I want to hold you. You're soft and warm, full of sparky nonsense and alluring bewilderment. You're the perfect antidote to a day at the hospital. You look at me as if I've hypnotised you, and you've got a dangerous way of making me feel like a giant.' He put his hand to her cheek, cupping the velvet softness and then stroking his fingers along her tender jawline. 'I look forward to coming home to you. Do you know that? It's like having an enchanting secret, my own princess in the tower. Maybe I'll keep you locked up here for ever.'

The things he was saying, the deep dark quality of his voice had already seduced Erica into a sort of trance and when his hand began to stroke her hair she drew up her slender legs and curled against him, accepting his right to hold her and enjoy her soft warmth. He sighed and relaxed as he felt her instant submission, his head leaning back against the chair, and she knew without looking that his eyes were closed. He needed her and it was thrilling, almost like a dream.

'Are you going to leap up and run away?' he asked quietly, and Erica shook her head, too filled with emotion to speak aloud. She snuggled her face against his chest and Alex's hand began to move over her slowly, almost absentmindedly. Her legs were curled up in the chair and his wandering hand found her ankle, his fingers caressing it soothingly.

'You've got pretty toes,' he murmured. 'Perfect enough to make a painting.' His fingers stroked over each toe slowly and Erica shivered with pleasure, astonished that such a strange gesture should bring her so much delight. Even his dark, quiet laughter didn't alarm her and her hand came to his chest, resting like a timid bird against the beat of his heart.

He bent his head, his lips brushing against her hot cheek as his hand covered hers.

'Do you want to touch me?' he asked huskily. 'Do you?' he repeated when she had no courage to reply.

Erica looked up at him, her blue eyes helplessly held by the dark gaze, and his eyes flashed over her face, sparks of light at the back of the darkness. His lips brushed hers and she found her hand placed against the warmth of his skin as he opened more buttons and held her hand beneath his, encouraging her to make this intimate gesture.

She gasped with a sort of wonder as her fingers spread out against his chest, feeling the beat of his heart, her fingertips exploring the hard masculine warmth. She had never touched anyone before. The thought had never been allowed to creep into her head. Too much fear and disgust had been embedded in her memory for her even to consider such a thing, but now her mind soared into forbidden delight and she was not even aware of the small murmur of pleasure that escaped her parted lips.

'Is it so good?' he whispered against her ear, his teeth lightly biting the velvet softness of her lobe. 'You're good for me too, Erica. I need your warmth. I need the feel of you against me.'

His words excited her even more and Erica's hand slid beneath his shirt to explore the strong muscles of his shoulder. Her breathing was fast and uneven. She was utterly entranced, completely without experience. The fact that she had shied away from any sort of masculine contact made her even more vulnerable and she was totally unaware of any danger that could ensue from this naïve exploration of such a virile, powerful man.

She heard Alex's gasp of pleasure and his strong fingers tilted her face, his eyes narrowing at the innocent fascination he saw in her wide blue eyes. He bent his head, his lips nuzzling sensuously against her neck, and she threw back her head with such submissive rapture that he made a low sound of masculine triumph deep in his throat and caught her lips with his.

It was like a flash of flame. Trembling feelings shot all over her and she melted against him, her arm sliding round his neck as her hand refused to be parted from the heated pleasure of his skin. His arm tightened around her and Erica felt nothing but yearning rapture as his hand began to explore her body with an urgency that would have sent a clear message to any other woman.

When he lifted his head she reached towards him, her lips softly parted, throbbing from the intensity of the kiss, and he parted her robe with the same urgency as he sought the soft, submissive warmth of her body.

'You've never done this before, have you?' he asked hoarsely, and Erica shook her head slowly, her eyes still on the tempting hardness of his mouth. She felt his hesitation but the feelings were so new, so beguiling that she looked at him with drowsy bewilderment and his lips fastened on hers once more as he claimed the sweetness of her mouth and clasped her close beneath the thickness of her robe.

When his hand closed over her breast, Erica gave a small whimper of frightened excitement and Alex raised his head to look deeply into her eyes.

'Tell me to stop,' he commanded thickly, his hand moulding her breast, and when she made the same plaintive sound his fingers brushed over the sharply raised centre, his eyes watching her shivering reaction. He lowered his head, his lips finding the place where his hand rested, teasing her aroused breast through the silken fabric of her nightie, and Erica jerked in his arms, a wild little cry leaving her that brought his lips back to hers swiftly.

He crushed her against him, his tongue invading the dark, sweet warmth of her mouth in a passionate kiss that left her weak and helpless. She was molten in his embrace, completely at his mercy, and when he turned his head and drew back Erica felt bereft.

'No,' he said almost violently. 'Whatever else I am, I'm not a villain.'

Erica looked at him in bewilderment. It was like being thrown out of paradise, and the hurt in her eyes only brought more determination to his face.

'I'm not even sure if you knew where that was leading,' he said thickly. 'You're a peculiar mixture of temper and innocence, woman and child. I don't even know who you are.'

Erica looked away, unable for the moment to get up and be at all normal. She was trembling with reaction, aching inside with a wild longing for something she had never even imagined in her whole life before. Tears came to her eyes and she hung her head, facing him almost accusingly when he tilted her chin and made her look at him.

'I want you, Erica,' he muttered unevenly. 'I wasn't even sure if I had the strength to say no just then. We're all alone. There's nothing to prevent me from carrying you to my room and my bed and that's exactly what I want to do.' His fingers explored the tears that slid down her cheeks but he didn't attempt to dry them; instead he watched them with a sort of hard fascination. 'Crying for me?' he asked softly. 'Tomorrow you would be crying for yourself, hating yourself.'

She stirred fretfully and he put her on her feet, steadying her and then standing to look down at her.

'I started all this because I needed your warmth,' he told her quietly. 'I also had to stop it because I have no idea who you are or why you're here.'

'You know why,' Erica whispered, hiding her face as she wiped at the fast-falling tears.

'Do I?' He lifted her face, his hands cupping her cheeks as he looked deeply into her eyes. 'I know what you say, beautiful Erica, but it's not the truth. One day I'll know the truth, but by then you may very well be a long way from here and completely out of my reach.'

Erica turned and almost ran from the room and he made no attempt to stop her. He would never know the truth. She could not let anyone find out and, most of all, Alex must never know. It was better to remain a mystery, someone to intrigue him, someone who would go from his life and leave just a puzzle behind her that would never unravel.

She got into bed and buried her head in the pillows, her body throbbing with beautiful, painful yearnings she had never felt before. She had not lived on a desert island. She knew where things had been leading. Being chaste was not being utterly innocent and stupid. She turned and stared out of the window where the moonlight on the icy snow cast unearthly light into her room.

Nothing about Alex had repulsed her. She had wanted him to touch her, wanted to touch him and she knew deep inside that if she had belonged to him she would not have felt any shame or self-pity tomorrow as he had suggested. She loved him and that was why she had been so willing, so eager, where normally she would have screamed and fought.

If he found out all about her, if he ever knew why she was here, what her intentions had been before she had seen her father, he would be angry, disgusted. He would look at her with scorn and she would deserve it. As to her old fears, he must never know about those either. She had been left feeling worthless, dirty and it would spoil anything that could ever have been between Alex and her. He would hate it.

Erica sighed and closed her eyes. Dreaming was useless. Alex had wanted her, not loved her. There was Fiona already, a suitable match, eager and willing to be his wife. Did he make love to Fiona? Did he say that he needed her warmth? She turned her face back into the pillows and cried herself to sleep.

CHAPTER NINE

OVER the next few days, Erica did her best to avoid Alex. It was not too hard because he was very late the following night and then he had to go to Edinburgh for another conference. When her father came home the times of being alone with Alex would be gone. It was as well because the few accidental meetings with him in the house had been fraught with tension and even on the morning when he told her he would bring Philip back during the afternoon there was a cold look to his face that brought a shadow to Erica's eyes. He gave her the information in a tightly controlled voice and she bit at her lip and looked away.

'Will he be able to work or is he to continue resting?' she asked carefully. She had been hard at it herself since her father had gone and now she had almost finished the work that had been piled up when she had come here.

'He's all right,' Alex assured her in the same tight voice in which he had announced the news. 'I kept him in hospital until I was quite sure about that. Keeping him away from the study would be an impossibility. It was better to make him rest with nothing to lure him back to his book.'

'If you mean me—' Erica began, glancing up with hurt and accusing eyes, and he snapped at her immediately.

'I don't mean you! I said what I mean and I said it precisely. Stop looking for trouble where it doesn't exist. You have enough problems without inventing any more.'

It was so uncannily true and the harshness of his voice so painful that Erica turned away. There was nothing to say to him and standing there was pointless. He reached out and stopped her, his hand coming to her shoulder to spin her round almost roughly.

'I'm sorry,' he said in a driven voice. 'I don't usually take my frustrations out on other people. The trouble is that you're the source of every frustration I have.'

'If you want me to leave ...' Her voice was trembling and he swore under his breath, his hand tightening on her shoulder.

'I do not want you to leave! Every instinct I have tells me to reach out and gather you to me. My intelligence tells me to watch my step. Being in a battlefield of my own making is dangerous.' He looked down at her wide eyes and parted lips, his eyes running sensuously along the curve of her mouth. 'Especially when you look at me like that,' he finished thickly.

In spite of his admission of distrust he was drawing her steadily closer and Erica was powerless to offer any resistance. Only the timely arrival of Mrs Roberts made them break away from each other, and minutes later Alex had left for the hospital.

Nothing was going to get any better. Erica went to the study and closed the door, finding a small area of peace in which to recover. One day, Alex would lose his strong hold on his own desires and then it would be too late to tell him anything. He would find out later and hate himself. He would hate her too.

She began to clear the rest of the work, making ready for her father's arrival. Her time here was almost over. The paintings were finished and now there was only the remainder of the book. She hoped he would not just go on and on writing, because if he did she would have to desert him and she wanted to finish the book with him.

*   *   *

Three days later, work was well under way, everything back to normal, at least on the surface. With her father at home, Alex came home from the hospital at a more reasonable time and things were safe. They tried not to look at each other; at least, Erica tried. Alex's eyes seemed to be drawn to her completely against his will. It was like a highly dangerous game of hide and seek, like lightning across a dark sky. Feelings crackled in the air between them so much that at times Erica wondered why her father didn't notice.

There was a sudden and unexpected thaw. The tightly packed snow melted almost overnight and one morning Erica got up to find a rather fitful sun shining, the trees and hedges dripping to the sodden earth, a few patches of green showing as the snow melted away.

'Hmm! A lull,' her father predicted, standing at the study window and watching the scene with sceptical eyes. 'Don't let it fool you, Erica. It's going to be back. This is just to let people drop their guard, then it will strike again and catch them out.'

He made everything sound sinister and Erica looked up, laughing at him.

'You don't like cold weather much, do you?' she enquired wryly.

'I don't like it at all,' he confessed, sitting to get on with his task. 'As soon as I'm better, I'll be off like a shot.' He gave her an amused little glance. 'Want to come with me? Want to be the private secretary of a game warden and author?'

He was only joking but her heart leapt at the thought. He liked her enough to suggest taking her with him, even if it was only a casual joke. She smiled, keeping up the spirit of things.

'I'm too attached to England,' she lied easily. 'Besides, the animals would scare me to death. Mrs Roberts seems to think you feed them all by hand.'

It allowed them to end on a note of laughter but Erica ducked her head and got on with her typing immediately. There had been more in her mind than sudden joy when he had made his playful suggestion. She had instantly thought of Alex. Not too long ago she had been pondering on how impossible it was to track her father to Africa. Now she knew him and loved him but Alex was here. Alex was in England and Africa was far away.

Even if her father had known who she was and had wanted her to go back with him she knew she would not have gone. While she was in England she would know where Alex was, know he was at least seeing the same sky. If she never met him again she could never go very far away from him.

She begged the afternoon off and drove to the village. She was completely out of shampoo and talc. There were several things she wanted but she had no luck at all. It was either baby talc or nothing and the shampoo looked as if they had stored it for centuries. She rang back to the house to tell Mrs Roberts and her father not to worry and then she drove on. The motorway would be clear and she could get back fairly quickly.

As it turned out, Erica did her shopping and then spent much longer than she had intended wandering around and gazing into shop windows. She didn't really want to buy anything. She knew she was doing everything she could to take her thoughts off Alex, and it was utterly pointless. He simply refused to leave her mind for even a second.

When she began to go back it was getting dark and before long she was meeting heavier traffic, people hurrying home and driving along the motorway at a speed that would have been alarming even on a summer afternoon. Her father had distrusted the thaw and she knew it was getting colder and colder by the minute. Any one of these idiots could hit ice with no warning.

Apparently, somebody had. The traffic came to a halt and in front Erica could see police cars with their blue lights flashing, police out in the road desperately trying to get cars onto the other side of the motorway. They'd cleared a gap in the central reservation and one by one she saw cars pull across and turn back the way they had come.

She knew that something really bad had happened and when it was almost her turn to be escorted across to the other side, another police car came up swiftly from town, a Mercedes tucked in behind him. It was Alex. She could see the grim lines of his face as he passed. He had been going home and he was now on duty again, but this time for what?

'What is it?' She wound her window down as the policeman came up to her car.

'Accident, miss,' he told her curtly. 'A tanker over-turned. Move across quickly, please. If there's any sort of explosion—'

'I saw a doctor go past,' Erica insisted, her heart almost stopping at the thought of any danger to Alex.

'The driver's trapped. Now come along, miss. Move over to the northbound side. We've got to clear as much distance as possible from the accident.'

'I'm a nurse.' Erica got out of her car and began to move forward, shrugging her arm free when he reached out to stop her. 'Two people can manage better than one,' she pointed out sharply. 'I can help the doctor and speed things up.'

'I don't think—' he began, but Erica snapped at him quickly, making his mind up for him.

'Turn the other cars. I can't do a thing while I'm arguing with you.'

Her determination had him convinced—that and his obvious duty to clear people out of danger. He spoke into his radio and let her go and Erica ran along the road, her only clear thought to get to Alex. There were patches of ice but she managed to avoid them. Away from the other cars, with no traffic at all, it seemed uncannily quiet.

She could see the tanker almost at once. It was on its side, the wheels turned away from her. There was no sort of spillage at the moment that she could see but she didn't know what it was carrying. There were huge industrial complexes not too far away and it was sufficient to know that the police were worried enough to get traffic clear. There were no cars coming in the opposite direction now. The other side of the motorway had been closed. They had isolated the whole area and soon Alex would be here alone with only the police to stand and watch.

'Where is he?'

She stopped, getting her breath back as she faced the two policemen who were fairly close to the tanker.

'The doctor is under the cab with the driver, Nurse,' one of them said, and she had a moment's shock until she realised the speed with which they could communicate with each other. That was why the other policeman had spoken into his radio and these two didn't doubt her identity. She slid to the ground and crawled under the tanker cab, drawn to the place by the dull groans of pain she could hear.

Alex was holding a torch, struggling to get to his bag in the confined space, and she came to him silently, taking the torch from his hand and directing it on the bag.

'Thanks,' he muttered. 'I can't see a damned thing here. He needs morphine. His leg's trapped, broken too, I think.'

He dived into the bag and as he turned to hold the needle to the light he saw her.

'Erica! Oh, God! Get out of here!'

'When you do,' she insisted quietly. 'I'll hold the torch. You do the really important stuff.'

'This thing could go up at any moment,' he began urgently, and Erica looked at him evenly.

'I don't think you should tell the driver that. Let's just get him out. I'm not leaving.'

Alex stared at her for another precious second and then gave in. It was obvious that she would not move and there was little he could do other than hurry. He gave the injection and then, as the moaning stopped, they worked together to free the driver's leg. One of the policemen crawled in at the other side and little by little they managed to ease him out.

When she had wriggled back to the edge of the cab and managed to stand upright, Erica found an ambulance already speeding up the road. She felt light-headed and her feet slipped on the road. It was icy, as she had suspected, and one of the policemen grabbed her arm, saving her from a fall.

That was when Alex appeared and the grasp he took of her other arm was not nearly as considerate as the policeman's.

'I'll take her,' he said curtly. 'You can manage without me. The ambulance crew will get him to hospital. The leg seems to be broken but he's reasonably all right. I'll have a look at him when he gets there.'

'Thank you, Dr Thorne,' the policeman said before nodding to Erica. 'Nurse,' he acknowledged gratefully, and from the corner of her eye Erica saw Alex's eyes narrow dangerously.

He didn't speak. By now the main traffic was cleared, and they walked along in silence. He passed his car and headed for hers and Erica tried to ease his grip on her arm.

'I can manage,' she began, but he ignored her, not even bothering to answer. It was only as they came to her car that he looked at her and she had never seen his face so forbidding. He still didn't say a word, and as Erica turned the car and crossed to the other side she saw him walking back to the Mercedes. She watched him in the mirror, saw him turn and leave the site of the accident behind him. He was safe. That was when the delayed shock hit her.

She began to tremble and all the rest of the way back to the house she had to keep a tight grip on herself to drive at all. Once, she had to stop for a minute but she knew it was not a good idea. If she delayed much longer she would not be able to move. At the front of her mind were terrifying pictures—a raging explosion, leaping flames and Alex in the middle of it alone.

She could not eat any dinner and she had the difficult task of telling her father about the accident. Not that she admitted her part in it.

She kept her voice steady. 'There was an accident on the motorway,' she explained when he looked worried at her lack of appetite. She had managed to slip upstairs when she had come in so at least she was not covered with oil and mud as she had been when she had first come back. Even Mrs Roberts hadn't seen her come in like that.

'Erica!' Her father looked at her anxiously, and she smiled her reassurance.

'I wasn't in it. We were stopped and turned back and I had to come the long way round. Alex was there,' she added, wondering fearfully what he would say when he got back.

He didn't come back for a long time and by then she had escaped to her room, Mrs Roberts had gone and her father had gone to bed. She heard Alex's car but this time she would not have dared to go down to face him. She went to have a shower and considered herself truly lucky when she came out and found her room still empty. The last look she had seen on Alex's face had warned her that he was more angry than he had ever been and she would not have been too surprised to find him standing thunderously in her room.

A few minutes later, he was! He didn't bother to knock. He came in with silent, menacing footsteps and the fact that he had changed his clothes and was still determined to corner her warned Erica that this time she would not get off easily at all.

'Nothing you can say will excuse your behaviour this time,' he grated, closing the door and advancing with an angry quiet that frightened her. 'Are you so determined to get a thrill that you're prepared to put your life at risk?'

'I wasn't trying to get a thrill,' Erica protested stiffly, backing away from him. 'I wanted to help.'

'So you told them you were a nurse and, being harassed enough as it was, they believed you.' He looked at her scornfully. 'You never have any trouble with lies, do you?'

'Not when it's necessary,' Erica admitted shakily, and anger flared over his face as he reached forward and grasped her arms.

'Necessary? If you hadn't forced your way in there, one of the police would have come to hold the torch and help me.'

'So why didn't he?' Erica was stung to reply. 'Why didn't you ask one of them for help?'

'Because the whole damned thing might have gone up at any moment,' he rasped. 'That was petrol in there! Nobody knew if the tanker skin was breached or not. I didn't want any other lives at risk. Next time you try some wildly impetuous scheme, check the situation out first.'

'I knew there might be an explosion,' Erica told him quietly. 'The policeman warned me.'

'You really knew?' Alex looked at her as if he doubted her sanity. 'So why the hell did you lie your way into there?'

'*You* were there!' Erica cried, bursting into a storm of tears. 'What was I supposed to do, turn and drive off and listen for the big bang? If you were going to be blown sky-high then I wanted...'

His stillness was an almost tangible thing and Erica wept quietly, too shaken to say more.

'If I was going to be blown sky-high you wanted to be with me?' he asked softly.

'Yes!' Erica wept angrily. She pulled away and turned her back on him but his arms came round her at once and he spun her back to face him, his eyes travelling over her tear-drenched face with a sort of startled wonder before he crushed her close and found her trembling lips with his own.

'Erica!' he groaned between heated, passionate kisses. 'You crazy, wonderful girl. Do you know I've been driving round the countryside, trying to recover from the fright of having you there in danger?'

'Is that why you're so late?' Erica looked up at him. There were still tears on her face and she was trembling more than ever. 'I thought the driver...'

'A broken leg and shock. He didn't need me at the hospital; in fact I'm not sure if he had as much shock as I had.' He cupped her face in his hands, his thumbs gently wiping her tears away. 'You scared me, Erica. I had this terrible image of you being killed.'

'That's how I felt when I knew you were under that cab,' Erica reminded him with a catch in her voice. 'I thought that before I could get to you it would explode. It took me a long time to run along the road. They were turning people away so quickly. It was like some terrible countdown.' Tears came back into her eyes and Alex looked down at her vibrantly.

'Don't cry,' he begged huskily. 'Don't cry, sweetheart. Nothing happened. We're both safe.'

'Please don't do it again, Alex,' she sobbed. 'I couldn't bear it if—'

'Shh! I'm here,' he whispered urgently. 'We're both here and nothing else matters.'

His lips sought hers, at first gently probing, but a shudder ran through his whole body at her feverish response. Her arms wound around his neck, little murmurs of distress escaping from her lips and Alex clasped her almost cruelly tight, moulding her against him as she clung to him in a frantic way, kissing him back distractedly.

'Even if I never see you again,' she sobbed. 'Even if you hate me—'

'Hate you? Oh, God, Erica! You're never out of my mind.'

He swept her into a world of sensation and delight, his voice whispering to her huskily, his hands moving over her with growing urgency. The thickness of her robe was too much to bear and it slid to the floor as Alex's hands closed around the soft, willing body that was pressed so close to his own.

'You're mine, Erica, aren't you?' he asked hoarsely, and her head fell back with total surrender.

'Yes,' she murmured drowsily. 'I don't know what else to be. When I've gone away—'

'No!' Alex's fingers bit into her, his hand cupping her head. 'I'll never let you go away. If you left I'd search for you for ever. I wouldn't do anything else with my life. I need your warmth, your soft body, your crazy adoration.'

He tilted her face, his lips nuzzling against the silken length of her neck, and Erica moaned as his lips moved to the swollen curves of her breasts. Her fingers clenched in his thick dark hair and Alex's breathing became erratic as he swung her up into his arms and placed her on the softness of the bed.

'I want to take you with me,' he said unevenly, 'but my room is too far away.' He came down beside her, pulling her into his arms. 'Don't be frightened, sweetheart,' he whispered. 'I won't hurt you.'

She wasn't frightened, not with Alex. That was something she already knew, a miracle. When he touched her now there was no memory of other hateful hands; she only felt Alex's hands, cool, strong and skilful, thrilling. She gave a little whimper of sound and moved closer but he held her away, his hands stroking her nightie from her shoulders, his dark eyes burning over every part of her he uncovered.

'You seem so small to me,' he breathed raggedly. 'Shining red hair like dark wine, creamy skin, and so willing when I hold you.' His glance moved like fire over her body. 'I want to own you, Erica, to make you part of me.'

He moved away, shedding his clothes, dropping them to the floor by the bed, his moody glance never leaving her, and when Erica came back to him with a wild cry of pleasure his lips covered hers in a searing kiss that carried them both far away from the lamplit room.

'Never be afraid of me,' he murmured intensely against her skin, his lips making rings of fire around her breasts, and Erica pressed against him, moaning with rapture.

'I'm not afraid,' she whispered distractedly. 'For the first time in my life I'm free.'

He moved over her, a slow, sensuous smile coming to his lips when he felt her body beneath him, and Erica's blue eyes widened in wonder at the joy she felt. A hard, masculine body was close to hers and all she could feel was swiftly mounting pleasure. She wound her legs round his, her hands stroking his face, her mouth hungrily seeking his kisses, and Alex's hands shaped her body as he moulded her even closer.

His caresses made her cry out in excited frustration and every bit of adoration she felt for him was clear in the hurried, anguished kisses she placed on his face and lips.

'Alex!' she moaned, her voice like a silver shadow of sound, and he knew the crest of desire that carried her along. He looked into her frantic eyes and closed his lips over hers.

'Now, my wonderful Erica,' he promised huskily.

She leapt in his arms as joy surged through her but he held her fast, murmuring encouragement against her parted lips until a glowing world of rapture enclosed her. Alex smiled into her eyes as he felt the soft relaxation spread through her and then his mouth claimed hers as he took her far from the room, far from the dark house that looked out on the icy countryside.

Stars leapt around her, touching her lightly, entering her mind. Together they floated through velvet blackness to bright, shimmering lights and then drifted back to earth clasped in each other's arms.

Erica opened her eyes minutes later and felt a great surge of shyness. He was hovering over her, watching her, and his fingers smoothed back her hair from her hot face.

'Am I still your hero?' he asked with amused gentleness, and Erica's eyes avoided his. It was impossible to believe. Her breathing was still uneven. She was trembling madly and Alex still held her close. She gave him a wistful look and he grinned at her, moving onto his side and curling her against him.

'What to do next is a problem,' he murmured. 'Do we stay here or go to my room?'

'Alex,' Erica managed uneasily, and he cupped her head in his hand, bringing it to his shoulder.

'Don't send me away,' he said softly. 'I would most certainly find myself coming back.' He looked down at her, tilting her face to his. 'You and I have got a lot of talking to do, Erica—unless you can simply forget what happened just now?'

'No,' she whispered, all her feeling very clear in the wide blue of her eyes. 'I'll never forget.'

He smiled down at her and then pulled the sheets over both of them.

'See that you don't,' he ordered. 'We have to sleep now. It's been a long, wonderful day.'

'Are you hungry?' Erica asked earnestly, remembering he hadn't come back for the evening meal.

'Not any more,' he laughed, pulling her close and switching off the lamp.

The whole room went dark and soon she could hear Alex's deep, steady breathing. He had gone to sleep holding her and she felt as if she had been touched by some bewildering miracle. She felt healed, safe, and even though she knew this could not last at all she had a small piece of happiness to carry with her for the rest of her life.

Cold moonlight flooded into the room and Erica gave a little sigh, snuggling closer to him. He moved to accept her warmth, his arms tightening, and she slept with no worries. Tomorrow would take care of itself. At least she had tonight.

Next day there was brilliant sunshine. Erica felt it on her face even before she opened her eyes. There was still the same languorous warmth about her, the memory of last night colouring each movement she made. She turned her head to look for Alex, wanting to watch him while he slept, but he was not there and she felt a moment of panic.

Maybe it had all been a dream? Did she love him so much that she could dream up enough bliss to make her feel as she did this morning? She gave a small, tragic sigh, her lips drooping unhappily, but her head turned sharply as a voice from the doorway spoke to her in an amused and almost tender way.

'Somebody had to get up,' Alex pointed out quietly. 'Quite obviously it had to be me.'

He was already dressed, ready to go to work, and Erica's cheeks flushed as she thought of the night before. Even now it seemed unreal. She couldn't think of one good reason why Alex should want her. He looked so wonderful—too important to spend any time at all with her.

'Come down to breakfast with me,' he ordered when she just stared at him desperately, and then his smile turned rueful as he came in and closed the door quietly.

'On second thoughts, wait until I've gone. Philip is no fool. He would only have to look at your face to know what had happened.'

He came to sit beside her and Erica shrank under the sheets. Her nightie was still at the bottom of the bed and there was no way she could reach it. Shyness threatened to choke her and Alex leaned over and collected it, placing it close to her.

'All right, if you really want this,' he said wryly. 'It's too late to hide, though.' His glance flared over her face, his looks serious and intent. 'When I come back this evening, you'll talk to me, Erica,' he told her firmly. 'I want to know a good deal more about you than I do already. Whatever you're hiding, whatever worries you have, I want to know.'

'I can never...' Erica began tremulously, and he tilted her face, looking deeply into her eyes.

'Last night you gave me the right to know,' he said quietly. 'You were an innocent, not just some girl who sleeps with anyone who happens to be there. I know all about fear and I've seen your fear come and go.' He took her face in his hands and smiled at her, his stern looks vanishing. 'You were afraid of men and yet you were willing to belong to me. Why?'

'I—I'm not afraid of men,' she managed quickly. 'In any case, I wanted to and—and...'

'And I didn't give you a great deal of choice.' He pulled her close, burying his face against her hair. 'Nobody has ever been prepared to die with me before, Erica,' he murmured softly. He gave a shaken sigh and trailed kisses gently across her face. 'You're the warmest, most loving girl I've ever known.'

Erica wanted to cling to him but she managed to hold back. He had said nothing to make her feel that this was in any way permanent. It could not be, after all. She was completely outside his life and she had too many dark secrets. If he knew, he would not think of her as he did now.

Alex drew back and looked at her.

'No warmth for me this morning?' he asked quizzically. 'What happened to those clinging arms?'

'I feel embarrassed,' she whispered. 'And you're in my room. If anyone comes in...'

'*Do* they come in?' he asked with mocking astonishment. 'I'll have to investigate that.' He stood and looked down at her, a teasing smile back on his face. 'All right. I'll have to manage without a morning kiss. Pity, I was hoping to persuade you to take Charlie out for me. I'm late.'

'I will,' Erica assured him eagerly, but he just nodded and turned to the door. 'Alex,' she called softly, 'I can't tell you the things you want to know. Please don't ask me.'

'I'm not going to. I'm late, as I told you.' He turned to look at her levelly. 'I intend to ask you tonight, though, and I intend to get some answers. Whatever happens at the hospital, I'll be here early, so get your story ready, Erica. Tonight we sort things out.'

He had gone before she could protest further and Erica pulled on her dressing gown and straightened up the bed. Shivers ran over her as she thought of last night. It could never happen again. Soon she would have to leave, and if Alex really meant to question her more closely tonight then she would have to defy him. It was either that or more lies. She could never tell him the truth.

CHAPTER TEN

WHEN the afternoon came around, Erica was still tossed between dreams and panic. This time Alex intended to find out the truth, and even if she was prepared to defy him she knew that sooner or later he would win. Whatever their relationship was, he now had the right to know, as he had told her this morning, but equally she dared not tell him. She could never face the accusation and anger that would show in his eyes when he found out all about her. As to her past life, there might be pity, and she did not want pity.

It was hard to believe that Alex simply wanted an affair with her. Her adoration of him would not allow such a thought to linger in her mind. All the same, he had said nothing, and even if he had she knew it could never have been a permanent relationship. Fiona was the one who was suitable and Alex would have to think about that. Passion was not nearly enough to base a whole life upon.

Since he had been in hospital, her father had agreed to rest in bed after lunch each day, and when he was safely settled Mrs Roberts came in with some late mail.

'I don't know what happened to the post this morning,' she said, shaking her head at such tardiness. 'It's just this minute arrived. I'll put Dr Thorne's on the hall table where he can get it when he comes home. This one is for Mr Macbride,' she added, glancing at it with interest. 'He hardly ever gets any English letters. He's been in Africa for so long that I expect most of his friends here have forgotten him. Can you put it on his desk, dear? He'll notice it there when he gets up. I'm going to nip over and give my cottage a clean-up before it's time to start dinner.'

Erica wasn't really listening. Her mind was still with Alex, still thrilled with the wonder of last night, still desperately trying to come up with some solution to her problems. She took the letter without much thought and it was only as she placed it on her father's desk in his study that her eyes fell on the envelope.

Cold waves washed over her, her mouth went dry and Erica sat abruptly in her father's chair and stared at the white envelope in front of her. She had no doubts at all. She had known that handwriting all her life. Her mother had written—but not to her. The letter was for Mr Philip Macbride. The postmark was from her home town. There was no room for hoping that it was a mistake.

Her mother had decided to carry out her threat and she had done it in the way most comfortable for herself. No journey into the snow-covered landscape of Northumberland for her. Writing a letter was much easier, and Erica had experience of the sort of letters her mother could write: she had received plenty of them herself on the subject of her neglect of her own home and her stepfather. Her mother's pen could drip poison when she desired and this one would have given her a wonderful opportunity.

There was no need to worry about not telling Alex. Now he would know and there was nothing she could do to stop the avalanche of knowledge that was about to descend on her father. This was her mother's forte and the letter was thick. It would be like a book of re-crimination and no stone would be left unturned. When he got up and opened this letter he would know everything.

For a few wasteful minutes Erica stood and stared out of the window but she was not seeing the parkland and the icily cold trees. Panic was racing inside her head, her thoughts colliding with each other, and even in her present state of mind Erica knew she must run. There was no alternative because she could not face either Alex or her father. She was too ashamed—ashamed of her original intentions when she had come here, ashamed of her silence as she had got to know her father. And she would never tell Alex about Jack Linton. That alone was a good enough reason simply to disappear.

As she went quietly up the stairs to pack her things, Erica felt almost numb. She knew what devastation she would leave behind. If she had simply gone before, her father would have been puzzled but now he would be hurt. She could have told Alex long ago. He had invited her to tell him more than once but she had drawn back, kept up the deceit, and now his contempt for her would wipe out all memory of last night.

She packed quickly, only pausing when she came to the things that Alex had bought her. Love for him washed over her as she folded the thick, winter clothes that he had so carefully brought home. She put her face against the white sweater, closing her eyes. She could not take them with her. She had no right to have them. It would seem like stealing because Alex would have bought her nothing at all if he had known her secret.

There was nobody to see her as she put her belongings into her car and moved off as quietly as possible. If her father was awake and had come to his bedroom window he would see her leaving but he could not stop her. In a few hours she would have managed to get far away and then she would be lost in London, back in her flat, back with the crowds on the busy streets, invisible. She would step back into her old life and never see Alex again.

* * *

As the last of the passengers left the plane, Erica walked slowly down the central aisle, checking to see that nobody had left precious possessions behind. There was usually something, from teddy bears to flight bags, and once somebody had forgotten a pair of fur boots—a startling discovery on a flight to Singapore.

This time there was nothing and as the crew left the flight deck Jeremy grinned at her happily.

'Back to the same routine?' he queried. 'It's just like old times.' It was. The two weeks since she had fled from Northumberland had dragged along. Now Erica didn't even imagine that she could see Alex in the crowds. She was safely hidden and even though he was never out of her thoughts at least she knew she would not have to face him.

He would never search for her. He was too aloof in his own world to sink to looking for her so that he could let her see his contempt at close quarters. Besides, he would have her father to comfort because the letter from her mother would surely have contained a blow that would have left any man shocked, and Philip was a sick man.

'Dinner tonight?' Jeremy asked as they walked with the others into the main building, but Erica shook her head. She didn't want to go out. If she stayed in her flat she could dream about Alex with no interruptions.

'I can't,' she murmured. 'I—I have things to do.'

'Like what?' Jeremy enquired drily. 'You've been saying that since you came back from Northumberland.' He glanced at her figure with a bleak look on his face. 'You've lost weight. You didn't have much to lose in the first place. That doctor up there should have been giving you a tonic instead of buying you clothes.'

'*Please!*' Erica said sharply. Nobody could speak of Alex. He was her secret and clinging to that was all she had left. She walked in with the others but Jeremy went silent after one speculating look at her tight face.

Her uniform made her look more slender still, with the cap perched attractively on her glowing red hair, the smart uniform jacket and the short skirt that showed off her long legs. She had acquired some sort of ethereal look while she had been up in the frozen north for those weeks. Her eyes looked too big and they never seemed to see anyone. She was pale under her light tan and on the short stopover she had refused to join in anything. She hadn't even been in the hotel pool.

As they stepped out into the open air, the cold hit them and they all reached for their top coats. It was December, well on the way to Christmas, and the change from one climate to another was always a shock.

'I often think about not coming back here,' one of the other stewardesses muttered. 'Just ponder on permanent sunshine. I could really live like that.'

Erica gave her a small smile. She had considered it herself, not for the sunshine but so that she could hide better. But Alex lived in England and even though she would never see him she had to know he was somewhere near.

They all turned away to their cars and Jeremy had one last try.

'Give me a break, Erica,' he begged quietly. 'If you want a shoulder to cry on then that's all right too.' He sounded quite depressed and Erica stopped, her hand coming to his arm sympathetically.

'I'm sorry,' she said softly. 'I can't ever . . . It's no use bothering about me, Jeremy.'

'A lost cause?' he asked astutely, looking down at her with serious eyes. 'Is he worth this misery, Erica?'

'Oh, yes,' she breathed, a sort of light shining suddenly in her eyes. 'He's wonderful. There's nobody in the whole world like him.'

'Then where is he?' Jeremy asked impatiently. 'Why is he letting you fade away like this? You're not even sufficiently in control of your mind to put your coat on. You're not even here at all, are you?'

Erica bit down on her lip and wondered how to answer. He was right, of course. She had been like somebody walking at the side of the world since she had come back. Everything she did was done automatically. Looking back now, she couldn't even remember the whole of the flight. She tried to speak but the words wouldn't leave her lips.

'Erica.' The voice was one she hadn't forgotten for one single moment and she stiffened, almost afraid that her dreams were taking on a reality, intruding into her everyday life. But Jeremy was scowling across at somebody and she turned slowly, her heart leaping into her mouth when she saw Alex standing there.

He was well protected from the cold, his sheepskin jacket over a dark suit, and there was that awesome splendour about him that always made her feel small and inadequate. She couldn't face him. She couldn't explain herself, excuse herself. She made a dive towards her car as Jeremy stood watching with astonishment on his face, but Alex was there before her, his hand gripping her arm.

'Oh, no, you don't!' he grated. 'My car, Erica. You don't leave my sight until I know what you're up to. Your days of dodging out of my way are over.'

Before she could speak, Jeremy was beside her, his face like thunder.

'Let go of her!' he ordered angrily. 'If you think you're dragging her off somewhere...'

Alex's dark eyes were turned on him coldly.

'I wouldn't harm a hair on her idiotic head,' he growled. 'I have no qualms about you, however.'

'Just try it!' Jeremy gripped her other arm and Erica had the alarming feeling that she was about to be taken off in two directions at once.

'Alex! Please!' she begged hopelessly, and Jeremy stopped at once, his keen glance moving over the other man's handsome, determined face, the possessive hand that still closed over Erica's arm.

'The "old" doctor,' he surmised, glancing at Erica wryly as he let her arm go.

'I'm ageing by the minute,' Alex muttered, his eyes skimming over Erica's shivering form. 'Hold her; she usually makes a run for it.' He slid out of his jacket and in a second it was round Erica's shoulders, its warmth enclosing her. Alex took charge then. 'You can leave her to me,' he said, nodding his thanks to Jeremy, who stood back with a rueful smile. 'She's tricky but I've got the hang of it now.'

'I can't come with you,' she began desperately. 'I don't want to tell you. I don't want to see you.'

'You haven't any choice,' Alex stated firmly. 'Walk or I carry you; either way, you're in my car in about two seconds. After that you might just have a small say in matters but no way do you leave my sight again.'

'Jeremy!' Erica said urgently, but he simply smiled at her in that same rueful manner.

'If this is the chap you've been pining for,' he pointed out, 'I'm not interfering. See you on the next flight—if he allows it.' He walked off, a quirky smile on his lips, and she supposed he thought that that was what friends were for. He didn't know anything about it. She was trapped with Alex now and his grip was crushing her arm.

'I haven't been pining,' she managed anxiously, and Alex shot her a black look before he turned and headed for his car, taking her with him at some speed.

'I have,' he muttered. 'You don't escape again, Erica. I know I'm landed with a madwoman but I'll try to do the thinking for both of us. We'll go to your flat,' he added as he forced her into the familiar silver car. 'Keep quiet until then. Spanking you here is just a bit too public and I'm quite well known in some circles. You never know who's watching.'

'My car!' Erica wailed.

'I'll have it collected later. Now be quiet,' Alex ordered.

'We can't go to my flat,' Erica managed at last when they had left the parking area and were speeding along the road. 'I won't take you there.'

'I'm taking *you* there,' he pointed out sardonically. 'It's bound to be more private than some hotel and I just might have to break all my vows and shout at you.'

'I'll not tell you where it is,' she threatened shakily, but Alex smiled disparagingly.

'I know where it is,' he informed her. 'I tracked you down from the flat. You used that address when you became a brilliant secretary. Now we're going back there, so keep quiet and think of a good excuse for your latest antics.'

'My—my flat's not nice enough to—to let you inside,' she whispered, and Alex grunted with annoyance.

'You live there,' he pointed out irascibly.

'It doesn't matter for me,' she began. 'You're different. It's not suitable for you to—'

'There's a lot of traffic,' Alex muttered, frowning at her for a second. 'If I brake and start to kiss you it might cause an accident. Stop this damned prince-and-scullery-maid attitude. If it's another trick then it's not working.

If you mean it, then I just might have to have your head examined. I want you to myself for a couple of hours. I want to say a lot of things to you and I want to hear why you suddenly fled. If we have to go into a coal shed to be alone then that's exactly what we'll do!'

After that he said nothing and Erica had not recovered from seeing him so suddenly to speak either. She wanted to turn and look at him, to glory in the fact that he was actually beside her but she dared not. By now he knew almost everything—unless her father hadn't told him. She looked at him with frightened eyes. Was that why he was here? Did he still want to know why she had left? Didn't he know who she was?

Erica was back to mindless panic and when he eventually stopped at her small flat she hung back until he took her bag impatiently and searched for her keys.

'You don't even give in to the inevitable, do you?' he grated. He opened the door and almost propelled her inside and before she could think of any further excuse the door was locked and the light was switched on.

'Small but neat,' Alex mused, looking around at her tiny but pretty little flat. 'A good place to go to earth.' He turned to look at her, his eyes skimming over her as she took off his warm jacket and stood there in her uniform, her eyes too big for her face. 'That's what we've done now,' he said quietly. 'We've gone to earth and we don't surface until I know every last thing about you, every secret thought in your head.'

'The—the letter...' Erica began, avoiding his eyes.

'I read it,' he told her evenly. 'It gave a new meaning to poison-pen letters. It was a blow to Philip but nothing like the blow he took when he discovered that you'd gone.'

'I never meant him to find out,' Erica said shakily. 'I was just going to finish the book and leave. I—I thought we might write to each other and—and perhaps be friends.'

'You and I?' Alex asked sardonically, and she looked up at him with accusing eyes.

'You know I mean my father!'

'But it's good to actually hear you say it,' he pointed out quietly. 'It didn't take Philip long to love you like a daughter, Erica, and then when he knew you really were his daughter you ran off.'

'He wouldn't want to know why I came there, why I tracked him down,' she cried bitterly. 'I blamed him. I came to spy on him and then confront him.'

'And it all went wrong,' Alex surmised quietly. 'You liked him.'

'He was ill. At first that stopped me. I would have gone right then, that first night, but I had no car.' She took off her cap and threw it on a chair, shaking her dark red hair free and sighing aloud. 'I couldn't seem to leave. I wanted to stay a bit longer with him.' She looked up pleadingly. 'I would never have told him, never have accused him of anything.'

'Oh, your mother did that very well,' Alex assured her grimly. He began to pace about, his hands in his pockets. 'There was a vicious undercurrent to the whole letter. It was designed to injure. I can understand the attraction that Africa had for Philip. It was a damned long way off. After a woman like that I would imagine a lion would be just a big, cuddly pussy-cat.' He glanced up and saw Erica's stricken face. 'You are not like your mother!' he said sharply. 'The letter was designed to injure you too.'

'What—what did she say about me?' Erica asked shakily. She dreaded to know but she had to ask him. So far all his anger had been directed at her mother but he would surely get around to her soon.

'She feels you've spent a good deal of your life looking for Philip and ignoring the people who really cared about you. According to her, you've shut yourself off from not only your mother but a kind and caring stepfather.'

Erica shuddered, closing her eyes and then looking down at her tightly clasped fingers.

'Maybe she feels like that with some good reason,' she whispered. 'She's my mother after all, and—and I went off as soon as I could. I never go home at all.'

'Remember what Fiona said so sweetly?' Alex asked quietly. 'Home is the place where the heart is. You ran away from home just over two weeks ago.' He sank down onto her small settee. It wasn't much bigger than one of Alex's chairs. 'Come here, waif,' he urged softly. 'You know perfectly well where you belong.'

'Alex?' Erica looked at him longingly, and the old, warm smile came back to his face as he watched her with dark, intent eyes.

'You look stunning in that uniform,' he murmured, his glance flaring over her, 'but it's very formal. I prefer the dressing gown, although the nightie would obviously be my first choice.'

Erica just looked at him, afraid to come any closer, and he held out his hand.

'Come to me, darling,' he said softly. 'There's no escaping from me so you may as well give in now.'

She came forward quietly, her eyes dazed and unbelieving. There was no anger on his face, no contempt, and when she was close he took her hand and pulled her down to his lap, his arms closing round her at once.

'Even in a uniform you're warm and soft,' he sighed. 'Oh, Erica! I missed you. Don't ever do that to me again.' He tilted her head back, his eyes roaming over her bewildered face. 'You're my secret,' he whispered. 'My princess in the tower. I couldn't even begin to manage without you. I love you and I'm taking you home.'

An incredulous smile lit up her face and her arms wound round his neck, clinging on tightly.

'Oh, I love you too, Alex,' she said with a catch in her voice, and she heard his warm chuckle.

'Well, I know that,' he told her in amusement. 'I watched you turn from being a very small but fierce marauder into a soft and gentle creature with adoring eyes.' He cupped her face with his hand and lifted it to look into her eyes then. 'I like being your hero,' he said softly. 'I like the way you wait for me to come home, the way you come softly into my arms. I like the way you melt into me, the feel of you beneath me, your little cries when I make love to you. I can't manage without you. I can't every try.'

His lips claimed hers, strong and possessive, and Erica felt every worried thought leave her mind. He loved her. He had said so and her lips parted willingly as she offered him all her sweetness, all her love. His hands skilfully removed her jacket even though his lips never left hers, and Erica murmured anxiously as her fingers sought to touch his skin.

'I know,' he said huskily, and his jacket joined hers on the floor as both of them worked feverishly at buttons in their desperation to get closer to each other. Erica's sigh when her hand was able to move over the hard warmth of his chest brought a flare of desire to Alex's dark eyes.

'I doubt if I'll ever get used to the way you need me,' he muttered thickly. 'You're all the warmth and passion in the world, wrapped up in one woman. Something hits me deep inside the moment I see you. I'm mad about you, Erica. I only have to look at you to want you. How

I managed all the time you were at the house, I don't know.'

He drew her blouse from her shoulders, his eyes intent on the beauty of her breasts beneath the white lace of her bra, and he buried his face close to her, his hands tightening when she threw back her head with a wild little cry of delight.

'Do you want me, darling?' he whispered against her skin as his fingers dealt with the small catch and her breasts were exposed to the heated rapture of his lips. 'These two weeks have been a lifetime. Let me love you.'

'I sleep through there,' Erica told him tremulously, her lips seeking his with desperate urgency, and he swept her up into his arms, carrying her like a feather through to her bed.

'We both sleep there,' he assured her huskily. 'We sleep there until I can breathe again, until I'm sure I have you back. Then I take you home.'

Tears came into her eyes and she looked at him with the same old adoration that she had never been able to hide.

'Home,' she whispered, tears sliding down her face as he finished undressing both of them.

'Wherever I am, you'll be there,' he promised fervently, clasping her close and collecting the tears with his lips. 'I'll never let us be parted again. If I have to go away you'll have to come and hang around waiting for me, but it had better be where I can look up and see you.'

He sounded so fierce that Erica smiled through her tears and touched his face with a sort of wonder.

'I'll probably mess everything up,' she surmised, and his face darkened as he looked into her eyes.

'Only if I have to walk out of a lecture to take you to bed,' he growled. He moved over her, pleasure flashing across his face as he felt the silken warmth of her body beneath his. 'If I go on feeling like this,' he whispered, 'I'll just stay at home with you, never let you out of my arms.'

She wound herself around him and he shuddered with pleasure, his lips seeking hers, crushing her mouth almost cruelly.

'Erica!' he groaned. 'You bring me to life. My adoring little angel, my sweet, mad girl. One day you'll understand how much I love you.'

They were locked in each other's arms, and Erica felt weak from his kisses, her skin burning, and when he possessed her she gave a keening little cry that made Alex's hands tighten in pleasure.

'Is it so good, my darling?' he asked thickly, and she called out his name, clinging to him as they soared off together into the brilliant lights and deep velvet of fulfilment.

Later as they lay together Erica thought of going back with Alex.

'How is my father?' she asked anxiously.

'Longing to see you, waiting for me to bring you home.' Alex stroked her face gently. 'He's so proud of you, sweetheart. He keeps on telling me how beautiful you are, how clever, and I keep telling him that I already know.' He looked at her intensely. 'He's a little worried that you'll be disappointed in him.'

'Disappointed? Why should I be? He's my father and I love him.'

'He left you to the mercy of that woman,' Alex pointed out grimly, and she shook her head, touching his face with so much love that he kissed every finger before he let her continue.

'He didn't know. Even my mother admitted that,' she pointed out. 'I was angry with him for no reason when

I set off to find him. I wanted to blame somebody and he was a ready-made scapegoat. But I didn't feel angry after I met him, not even on that first night. It wasn't long before I loved him—a sort of instinct, I expect.' She glanced at Alex and smiled. 'You almost guessed, didn't you?'

'It crossed my mind,' he admitted quietly. 'There was just something about both of you that seemed to be alike. The eyes, maybe, the way you laughed. Sometimes I felt quite left out.'

'Oh, Alex,' Erica laughed. 'From the very second day I used to watch for you coming home. If I hadn't been trying to hide my secrets—'

'Yes, secrets,' Alex said quietly when she suddenly stopped. 'There'll be no more secrets between you and me. Tell me about Jack Linton, Erica. Tell me about this stepfather you treat so badly, according to your mother.'

'There's nothing to tell,' Erica said sharply, turning away, but he turned her back to face him, locking her in his arms and tilting her face. It was suddenly pale, the flushed, wild beauty subdued.

'No secrets,' he ordered deeply. 'At first you were afraid, even with me. I saw the look in your eyes. What did he do to you, Erica?'

'Nothing,' she whispered, her eyes tightly closed, and he pulled her to his shoulder, his hand stroking her face.

'Tell me, my love,' he urged softly. 'Tell me and it will all go away.'

She gave a shaken sob but there were no tears. Now the face never imposed itself between her and Alex; now the thick, blunt fingers never came into her mind. Alex had made her whole, made her free and it didn't matter any more.

'He—he used to try to touch me,' she whispered. 'I was little and I hated it. I knew it was bad but he just laughed. He's a horrid man—big, a bully. Sometimes he shouted at me for nothing and my mother never interfered and sometimes—sometimes—' She stopped, her voice choked up, and Alex held her tightly.

'Go on, darling,' he said softly.

'When I was older, about sixteen, he used to follow me when I went out. He used to wait outside school sometimes and I had to go the back way, climbing over the fence in case he saw me. I knew I wasn't safe until I got home and I would never go in unless my mother was there. When he came in then he would be angry and I was the only one who knew why.'

'What did he do to you?' Alex asked, and there was so much fury in his voice that Erica reached out and touched his lips gently.

'Nothing,' she told him earnestly. 'He never had the chance, Alex, truly. I was too wary, too quick for him. I pulled the dressing table across my door at night and I was always careful. I was never alone with him. He used to get ugly and angry but I pretended to be startled and bewildered. He never dared say anything to me about that. He just paid me back in a million other ways. I went to college and it was such a relief, and when I was old enough I left home. I got a job in London and just stayed away. It infuriated both of them. Of course, my mother never understood.'

'Don't bank on it,' Alex ground out furiously. 'Even if she didn't, you were her daughter and she let that vile creature bully you.' He pulled her so close that she could scarcely breathe. 'Is that all, sweetheart? You're not keeping anything bottled up inside?'

'No, Alex,' she managed unevenly. 'I never wanted to tell you. I thought you might think I was... He made me feel unclean!' she burst out, and Alex eased his strong hold on her, leaning over her to look into her eyes.

'I think you're bright and beautiful,' he said clearly. 'I think you're the stars of the morning, the white, pure snow, the clear, clean waves of the sea. I think you're a miracle, my miracle, my princess. I love you so much that I could die happily with you in my arms.'

She started to cry then, tears and laughter mixed on her face as the last dark secret fled from her mind and he caught her close, kissing away her tears, covering her smiling mouth with his.

'My love,' he murmured huskily. 'My own sweet love.'

'After a minute, when she felt safe and secure, Alex looked at his watch and moved to get dressed.

'Let's go home,' he said firmly. 'I hate the city. It stifles me, and somewhere, lurking about, is that boy-friend of yours.'

'Jeremy?' Erica asked, looking up with startled eyes. 'He's not my boyfriend!'

'But does he know that?' Alex asked wryly, glancing at her sideways as he tucked his shirt into his trousers and tossed her her clothes. 'If you told him I was an old doctor, he might go on hoping.'

'Oh, that,' Erica muttered, her face flushing under his derisive stare. 'I mentioned that you'd bought me some clothes and he pounced on it. I told him you were a doctor-friend of my employer and old. It put him off the track. I was being secretive then.'

Alex laughed and pulled her from the bed into his arms.

'I expect you'll try to be secretive from time to time,' he surmised ruefully. 'It won't work for long. I told him I'd got the hang of it now. I can only improve. Get dressed, my little waif. I'm taking you home, back to your employer and then straight to my bed.'

Erica thought about Fiona as they sped northwards towards her father. When Fiona found out about this there would be trouble. She wanted Alex herself and she would never give up. Erica sighed and Alex was alert at once.

'Aloud, please,' he ordered. 'Clear English and straight to the point.'

'It's Fiona,' Erica admitted uneasily, and Alex glanced round with mocking surprise.

'Where?' he asked quickly. 'Did we pass her? I hope she didn't notice.'

'Don't tease me, Alex,' Erica muttered plaintively. 'Fiona wants to marry you. She told me she intended to.'

'I know,' Alex sighed. 'The trouble is, I could get into serious difficulties if I married two women, and I chose you. I expect she'll recover from the shock. She's been engaged to at least two men since she was twenty. She thinks it's my turn. It's her kindly, thoughtful way.'

He was grinning to himself but Erica hardly heard all his little speech. Her heart was thumping madly and she dared to ask the question that sprang to her lips.

'You're going to marry me?' she whispered.

'Oh, yes,' Alex said seriously. 'Your father lives in the same house. It would be tricky otherwise. In any case, I couldn't just have you for a mistress. I have a fabulous reputation, being heroic and important as you know quite well.'

'You're teasing!' Erica reproached him and he pulled off the road, diving into a lay-by and stopping, taking her in his arms and looking down into her face.

'Will you marry me, Erica?' he asked huskily. 'I can't live without you.'

'You're so wonderful, Alex,' Erica sighed, smiling up at him. 'Sometimes you're quite stern and at others...'

'And as a doctor I should know better?' he asked, stroking her face with gentle fingers. 'Say yes and we'll go back home. Say no and we'll return to your flat and stay there for the rest of our lives.'

'Yes,' Erica laughed, throwing her arms wildly round his neck. She suddenly looked serious and his smile faded.

'What is it?' he asked urgently.

'I've got a flight tomorrow.'

'Oh, that!' He started the car and turned back towards the north. 'You've left. I'll write an official letter and we'll parcel your uniform up and return it. If they protest, then you're very sick. I can vouch for that. You're definitely not fit to be let out; in fact you won't be let out in future without your keeper.'

'I suppose that's you?' Erica laughed, and he lifted her hand, kissing her fingers.

'Who else?' he asked softly. 'Have a rest now, my love, and when you open your eyes you'll be home.'

She closed her eyes obediently, her head coming to rest against his shoulder.

'I love you,' she murmured drowsily, and Alex's eyes flashed to her face, seeing the peace there, her soft lips curved in a smile. He had her safe at last. He felt fiercely protective, as he had done almost from the moment he had first seen her.

'Don't ever stop,' he said huskily, and she sighed, cuddling closer to him.

'How could I?' she asked simply. 'You're my world. All I ever want is to be near you.'

Alex smiled and headed homewards. It was beginning to get dark, the first signs of northern snow showing in a more barren landscape. In the summer it would be beautiful and she would still be there, running through the fields by the house, walking with him by the sea, wrapped in his arms each night. His adoring angel. His love.